MW01232658

Shadow of a Sinner

A Novella

Brandi Lei Morrison

I dedicate this short novel to those from my hometown
who connect with this story.

I thank my pre-release readers, Marsha, Braylon, Genia, Maurice, and Shimeka, for their time and commentary during the rough draft stage.

I thank Christopher, whose editorial expertise helped me grow as a writer and taught me to trust my readers.

I am grateful to my family and friends for their continued support, feedback, and encouragement throughout this writing journey.

PROLOGUE

OCTOBER 2023

The soft, early morning sun lit the abandoned park. The whistling of the wind alerted waking creatures, sending them scurrying, eager to start the day. The air swept the dusty fine gravel on the walking path, tossing it between the tangled legs of old trees. A white Audi sat at the back of the parking lot with its front windows partially down. A designer clutch sat on the passenger seat floor, and an unopened package rested on the backseat. An iPhone, face up, on the center console exposed a list of notifications that lit up the screen, flashing a selfie of a young woman with brown eyes and shoulder-length curly hair. The unanswered notifications were from her boss asking if she was still coming in to work her evening shift, a woman's voice singing Happy Birthday, a guy she met a couple of weeks ago at a club, and her mother who lived several states away and seldom communicated, asking about the gift and card filled with cash she sent again this year. The screen went dark.

An anxious driver pulled his truck into the parking lot, turning into a space that faced a set of worn bleachers and the backstop of a nearby softball field. He unlocked the doors, motioning for his passenger to exit. He had more important things to do. The things he did during the bright hours of the day: A quick chat with the café employee who handed over his usual boudin bacon kolache and a cup of caffeine, and the quick nod or two he managed as he wormed his way through the office maze, brushing past coworkers. A blend of work and play eased his day as he sent messages to others in the office, earning a high-pitched giggle from one or two cubicles. This morning's drop-off was just play, something he did for fun, with those who stayed in darker places. Spaces cloaked under thick branches, like the ones in the dimly lit park, buried deep under the crinkling leaves that swept the autumn floor.

Alexis Landry grabbed her purse, shoved the car door open, and stumbled onto the pavement, her long boxed braids swaying against her back. She caught a whiff of the unpleasantries that slithered past the cement walls of the park's restrooms. The ground was unsteady beneath her stiletto heels, and the trees invited her to swing out like the older men who retired to hole-in-the-wall night clubs. Her head was pounding. Alexis caught her breath as she shut the door. Her driver revved out of the lot heading toward the business-lined streets of the Oil Center. He didn't care if she made it to her car. After the dust settled from the disturbance of screeching tires, she heard her phone ding. She unlocked the screen to read the text from her one-night stand.

Thanks. C u around.

Bastard!

lol

"Bastard," she muttered. Alexis pulled down on her mini skirt, which was useless against the biting chill, pricking her long bare legs. She regretted not wearing pants, helplessly hugging herself in the sleeves of her pullover sweater. She opened the car door and tossed her worn purse inside the Nissan when she heard a notification that wasn't hers. The alert went off again, this time chiming louder. She wanted to go home and wash off the dismissive man's stench. The noise blared again, turning her attention towards a nearby white Audi. She glanced inside the neighboring car and spotted the nuisance: an iPhone, a new edition. She reached in to retrieve it when she spotted a Chanel handbag on the passenger seat floor. She walked around the vehicle and opened the door. The high-end handbag had a matching wallet full of cash. Alexis studied the driver's license of a woman about the same age. At the bottom of the purse was a light green object with a logo that said HAVEN, embossed in dark green ink, written in all caps. Alexis fiddled with the shiny medallion as she slid the cash into her bra. She returned to her car, Chanel bag in hand, cash tightly secured against her chest.

Rustling leaves and what sounded like a squeal made her stumble. She pressed her hands against the trunk to keep from falling. The noise came from a nearby tree at the back of the lot. Alexis dismissed it as a squirrel or other fury being that she didn't want to get acquainted with when she spotted the tip of a boot poking out from the tree's base. Tiny bumps sprouted on her forearms. She wanted to run to her car, but sore feet wouldn't allow

6

it. Alexis closed her eyes, wishing herself away under her bed sheets and lush comforter. She looked at the image of the young woman on the driver's license again.

She approached the tree and saw the dusty denim pant leg connected to the cognac-colored bootie. The hives spread up her arms, making their way to her neck as she took in the lifeless body of the woman. "No, no, no..." Alexis took a few steps backward, attempting to shake the image out of her head. Her legs gave way, and she fell to the ground, crushing small branches beneath her, twigs stabbing the palms of her hands. The woman trembled as she struggled to stand, running back to her car. The ID slipped through her fingers, landing face up on the ground.

The dead woman's body sat up against the tree's thick, crawling legs that sprawled out into a tangled web of claws that could grab and pull you in at any moment. She was leaning slightly to one side, resembling a doll on a shelf, in dusty dark denim skinny jeans, a fitted square-neck burgundy top, and jacket. A silver circle pendant with the letter B rested between her tan breasts, and her full head of soft brown ringlets sat above her shoulders. Her wide almond eyes stared at the empty field.

Alexis pulled into a parking spot in front of her apartment on the second floor of a neglected four-plex. She managed the one flight of stairs one dazed step at a time. On the first couple of tries, her shaky hands fought the keys to unlock the door. Once she stepped into the safe walls of her apartment, she tossed her purse and the designer bag on the sofa and threw the keys on the kitchen counter. Sitting on the tub's edge, Alexis leaned over to

turn the squeaky faucet before returning to the bedroom
to kick off her stilettos and strip out of her clothes. She
heard a ringtone from the living room and then a double
ding moments later. Alexis saw the woman's phone. She
thought quickly, hurried to turn it off, throwing the iPhone
back on the sofa like it could scar her hand. She returned
to her bedroom and launched her dirty clothes toward the
laundry basket, not caring where they landed. The water in
the shower ran cold. She reached for the screwdriver in
the bathroom cabinet and smacked the pipe several times
to scare some heat into it. Alexis stood naked, crying,
watching the warm water wash her sins down the drain.

CHAPTER 1

JUNE 1995

"I want a love like that." Nine-year-old Chelsea Richard stared at a young couple holding hands on the beach. The teenage girl wore short white cuffed denim shorts and a gold crop top with her hair in a high ponytail and bangs. Her companion sported a baseball cap, two-tone Bermuda-style shorts, and a plain white t-shirt. He leaned over to kiss her as a group of guys in swim trunks walked past.

Chelsea thought the couple looked cute together. She and her just-turned-thirteen-year-old sister, Charla, waited in line for waffle cones at their favorite creamery.

"What did you say?" Charla asked, staring at the teenage worker as she carefully shoved the ice cream into their cones.

"When I have a boyfriend, I want a relationship like theirs." Chelsea nodded toward the couple.

"You better look again." Charla studied the teenagers. "There's trouble in that paradise."

The couple walked towards the ice cream shop and stopped as they approached a bench.

"I wasn't looking at them, okay!" The girl pulled away from her boyfriend. Her body language shifted from the previous nurturing movements.

"I saw you." The boy grabbed her arm. She attempted to pull away again, but he had a firm grip.

"They're a group of friends from school." She paused, her face reddening. "You look at girls all the time..."

Charla turned her younger sister away from the couple. "Things aren't always what they seem."

"You like to ruin everything." Chelsea stared at the parlor counter, avoiding eye contact with her sister.

"No, you're just being naïve."

"I have an order for half vanilla, half pecan praline, and a Neapolitan!" The employee called out with a smile, proud of her creation.

Chelsea stood still. Charla pushed past her sister and took both cones from the cheery female. Chelsea trailed behind as they walked out of the creamery, hanging her head down. Charla handed a cone to her sister.

"I just want you to see the truth, okay?"

"Yeah, okay," Chelsea mumbled as she took her ice cream. The vanilla and pecan praline mixed with the cinnamon waffle cone sweetened her mood slightly.

The sisters walked towards the main beach parking lot that sported a giant beach ball on top of a pole. After a few minutes of maneuvering through parked cars, they spotted their parents loading the trunk of their SUV. Chelsea called out to their mother, Helena.

"Hi, my babies."

"Hey, mom." They replied.

"I see you stopped by the ice cream shop."

"Yes. The line was crazy long, and the workers were slow." Charla complained.

"You want some of mine?" Chelsea offered their mother.

"No, sweetie. I don't want to make your father jealous." She giggled, nudging her husband. "You know he can't have it anymore."

"Have some if you want, my dear." Their father, Charles, called out as he put the last of the bags in the trunk.

Chelsea looked over at her mother, but Helena shrugged the cone away. She went back to enjoying her treat. Her mother reached out to hold their father's hand.

Every summer, their family took a trip to the beach. After their father purchased a rental property in Pensacola, Florida, he ensured the family visited every summer. Days leading up to our trip, he made several calls to family and friends, alerting them of our absence over the next several days.

"Let's roll!" Their father closed the trunk and motioned for everyone to enter the vehicle. "I hope that ice cream doesn't spoil your appetites. I'm grilling burgers tonight."

Chelsea patted her stomach. "I'm up for it."

"You're always up for some food." Charla teased, earning her a shove from her sister.

"That reminds me, Charles," their mother looked up from the magazine in her lap, "we need to stop by the store to get potatoes for the fries, ketchup, and mayo."

"I'll drop you ladies off so you can get cleaned up and cooled off in the a/c. I can go to the store after I run this baby through the carwash."

"Works for me." Helena looked out the window before looking back down at the magazine.

Once they arrived, they hauled the bags into the house. After the family emptied the vehicle, Charla stood in the living room under the air vent, sighing relief. She noticed her sister went straight to the bedroom. Chelsea hadn't spoken more than a few words to her on the ride home. She left her cooling spot.

"You're still mad at me?" Charla stood in the doorway of the bedroom.

"Nope," Chelsea plopped down on the bed.

Charla sat down next to her younger sister. "Okay, well, maybe we can go visit Tara later?"

Tara and her family stayed in a house in the same neighborhood. She had a five-year-old brother, and the last time Chelsea visited, he conned her into playing hide and seek. Their families often ate together when the Richards came for the summer.

"I don't know. I think I'll stay here." Chelsea pulled a book from under her pillow.

"Suit yourself." Charla contemplated making another proposition but left her sister in her own space.

Charla heard bickering coming from the kitchen. When she entered, her mother leaned over the kitchen sink, holding her right arm close to her chest. Her father breathed heavily, standing a few feet from his wife.

"Is everything okay?" Charla broke the silence, startling them.

Her father cleared his throat and nodded, sliding a liquor bottle out of sight. Her mother spoke first. "Yes, sweetie. I just cut my hand on a glass in the sink. That's all." She looked over at her husband. "Can you bring me a Band-Aid, rubbing alcohol, and a paper towel, honey?"

"Yes, of course." He moved quickly towards the bathroom.

Charla noticed that her mother still hadn't turned to face her.

"Let me look at it." She walked over to her mother.

"No, it's okay." Helena rejected. "It's nothing." She wiped her face briefly with her other hand before smiling at her daughter.

Charla stood next to her mother and put her arm around her. Her father came back into the kitchen. He put the Band-Aid on the kitchen counter, folded the paper towel, and poured alcohol before running it under a light stream of water. He placed it inside her mother's hand.

"You should go before it gets late." She pulled her hand back from her husband and tended to her wound.

Charles nodded in agreement and grabbed the keys on the kitchen table. "I'll be back soon," he called out before walking out the front door.

Charla heard the SUV's engine. She went to the window to watch her father back cautiously out of the driveway.

Helena sat at the table of the summer house with her daughters; she just finished putting burgers on the plates with some chips she found in the pantry. Her husband still hadn't returned from the store, and she noticed a couple of cookies were missing from the fresh batch she took out of the oven. It was close to their bedtime. She let them watch a show after dinner while she cleaned up in the kitchen, scrubbing away the stains from their dishes and inspecting them as she wiped them dry.

Charles stumbled through the door, the smell of alcohol on his breath. The girls were already asleep.

"Where have you been?" Helena questioned when he entered the living room. "Are you drunk?"

"A man can't go have a drink?! Damn."

"Don't use that tone with me! We're on vacation; you should have been here for dinner."

"I had something I needed to do, alright." He didn't feel the need to elaborate.

"Like what?! What else is that important?" His wife snapped.

"Look, it's not a good time right now, okay! My head hurts."

"You're not getting out of this one."

"What are you talking about?"

"I found a number in your pants pocket."

"You're going through my things? You don't trust me?!"

"Looks like I had every right." He took a step towards her. "Don't come near me." She turned her nose up at the messy sight of her husband.

"Mom, Dad, what's going on?" Their youngest's soft, sleepy tone pressed the brakes on the fight.

"Nothing, sweetheart. Your father is about to shower before we go to bed."

"But I heard yelling."

"We just got a little loud, Chell, that's all. I'm sorry I missed dinner." Charles looked over at his daughter with a loving smile.

"Okay." Chelsea wiped her eyes and turned to go back to bed.

Once her daughter went back into the bedroom, Helena turned back to her wasted husband. "You can pull out the sofa bed when you're done."

Charla still had the covers pulled over her head when her sister walked back into the room, climbing back into bed. Not long after their father returned, she heard the fight but pretended to sleep when Chelsea started to stir, the raised voices disturbing her dreams. Charla thought about stopping her sister when she got out of bed, but she wanted Chelsea to see the cracks in their parents' relationship.

CHAPTER 2

OCTOBER 2023

CHARLA

"Ugh," I looked at the clock on my car media dashboard. I couldn't move without slamming on the brakes. I had been looking at the same house with green shudders and a red door for several minutes. A restaurant sign across the street advertised a deal on Ghost Wings. Driving in the narrow lanes on Pinhook Road always made me feel claustrophobic. I felt like the side mirror of a passing car could graze mine any minute if I didn't stay in the center of the lane.

"It's okay, Ma," my eight-year-old daughter, Delilah, called from the backseat. "You always get me to school on time."

"Early is best." I rebutted.

"I know. I know." Delilah whined in agreement.

I glanced at the rearview mirror to see her fiddling with the buckle clips on her purple backpack, which looked like it had been bathed in silver glitter. It took me thirty minutes too long to perfect the side jumbo ponytail as she saw on a character of one of her favorite shows. She didn't steal her big dark doe eyes, taking after her father. My baby grew out of the clothes from last school year; her thin, sharper facial features showed her age. The days of strapping her in the car seat and kissing her forehead before I got behind the wheel were gone.

Traffic started moving again, and I arrived at the school's car rider circle. I reached for my insulated tumbler and sipped on my homemade hazelnut cappuccino.

"Do you like my design?" Delilah asked.

She smiled at the sparkly stickers she stuck all over my container. "I love it, sweetie." I held it up with pride. Her ponytail bounced in delight.

We reached the elementary school, and I entered the front circle line. I turned up the music as the line moved quickly. My daughter held the backpack in her lap and reached for her matching lunchbox. "Don't undo that seatbelt until we are at a complete stop."

"Yes, ma'am," she recited.

When I stopped in front of the school, I heard the clicking sound of her seatbelt. She leaned forward to kiss me on the cheek.

"Bye, Ma!" Before I knew it, the backdoor opened, and Dede hopped out, ready to meet up with schoolmates and her third-grade teacher, who had morning duty.

"Bye, Nugget! Have a good day."

"Aww, ma," she complained. She hated it when I called her by her nickname around her friends.

I called her Nugget for as long as I could remember. During my pregnancy, I craved chicken nuggets with any kind of dipping sauce I could find.

I had twenty minutes to get to the office. I took another sip of my warm drink. I studied the scattered stickers made up of stars and hearts. It gave my sleek black tumbler character.

I pulled into the parking lot of the Robichaux & Moreau accounting firm. I parked the black Lexus in my usual spot a few spaces from the front door. A message popped up from Travis Morgan, a long-time friend since high school. He just wanted to check in since we hadn't spoken. I sent him a quick reply saying that I would call during a break. I walked through the front entrance with my purse, business tote, and bedazzled tumbler. Out of habit, I turned to say good morning to Tina, our receptionist, but the empty chair reminded me she was still on sick leave. I nodded to the few colleagues I spotted on the way to my office. The more extensive office suite next to mine belonged to my boss, Daniel Robichaux. He wouldn't return from his vacation for another week.

I had just put down my bags and sat at my desk, relieved to be out of traffic. I logged onto my computer and waited for the list of unread emails to load. Cindy, my senior accountant, knocked softly on my open door. She had a folder in her hand.

"Good morning, Charla. Happy Friday!" her chipper voice contrasted with her body language.

"Good morning, Cindy." I motioned for her to come in.

"I wanted to catch you before you got busy. It's about Aaron." She handed me the folder.

Aaron was a new hire and a staff accountant. He was also related to Tom Moreau, the firm's other partner. He had been working at the firm for a couple of months. I opened the folder and saw a form and invoice for a new client, Greener Earth, LLC.

"What happened with this account? I looked up at Cindy. "Why are we charging them this much for the listed services?"

"Aaron made an error when he entered Greener Earth into our system. He put incorrect fees for some of the services." She shook her head slowly. "Their assistant controller called yesterday after you left." She shook her head disapprovingly again. "I corrected it, of course, and did my best to smooth things over, but I wanted you to see what happened." Cindy, a suck-up, didn't like Aaron. She never admitted it, but she only spoke to him if it was work-related and avoided lunches that included him. I knew she secretly reveled in his mistakes.

"Thanks for bringing this to my attention and fixing the issue immediately. I'll reach out to the company if needed."

"Of course." She fidgeted with her hands in her lap. "I'm sure it's just an oversight on his part. We just can't risk mistakes like that happening again."

"I'll meet with him. Is he here today?"

"Yes." She quickly offered.

"Tell him to come and see me when you return to your desk."

"Okay, I'll do that." She rose from her seat and stood at the door. She completed her mission to rat on Aaron.

"Also, I would like you to schedule more training time with him."

"Yes, of course, I'll schedule it this morning."
Cindy exited. I noticed a little pep in her step as she
rushed to her side of the office, aiming straight for Aaron's
cubicle.

Aaron sat in the chair across from my desk. I
looked out my window to see Cindy creeping past for the
second time on her way to the copier. I discussed the
incident regarding Greener Earth.

"Yes, of course." He tossed his sleek, gelled hair
to one side; his lips formed a tight smile. He knew who
told. "My apologies; it'll never happen again."

"Mistakes happen. We all make them." I offered
some consolation. "We just need to keep it to a
minimum."

"Yes, absolutely." He nodded, letting me know he
understood.

I released Aaron to the office floor and asked him
to close my door. I needed to finalize some reports before
lunch. I checked my cell phone and saw that I missed a
call and message from my sister, Chelsea. She realized she
missed early voting and would probably have to stand in a
long line on election day. I sent her a quick text
apologizing and promised to call soon. Now, I had two
calls to make. I called Travis.

"Well, if it isn't Miss Busy Bee." He joked.

"Hey, jokester. I'm sorry. You know I have
mommy duties and work."

"Who are you telling? I have my little one for the
next two weeks, and these employees don't want to come
to work." Travis has a son close to Delilah's age and works
as a general manager in retail.

"How is Tristan doing?"

"Six going on forty."

"Dede is the same." We both laughed.

"What's been going on besides work and being supermom? A lucky man has you occupied?" Travis and I have always been best friends, but he liked asking about my dating life. I took too long to respond. "Ohh, so there is someone."

"Stop being nosey. There is someone, but it's fresh, so you know."

"I get it."

"What about you? You're all in my business. Aren't you seeing someone?"

"Not anymore." He stressed.

"I see." I reached for a pen on my desk and tapped it on my thigh, wondering how long it had been since the relationship ended. My office line rang, and I needed to take the call. Travis and I agreed to speak again soon before we got on with our workday.

CHAPTER 3

CHELSEA

I balanced my cell phone between my shoulder and ear as I tried to calm Marsha Thomson, my executive assistant and center manager. Her teenage energy disguised her early fifties age range. She reminded me of my Aunt Sellie. I sorted through paperwork that cluttered my office, and I'd made a decent dent in reducing the number of stacks. Sometimes, running a nonprofit organization that provides services for substance abuse recovery has more administrative challenges than the people we help. I lost my childhood best friend, Erika Simon, to substance abuse. It started during our first year in college at LSU. It began as a recreational activity at parties and other places. During her sophomore year, she took them to get through exams. By the Fall semester of our third year, she didn't go a day without them.

"I can stop whenever I want." Erika snapped at me one day, throwing her book sack against the wall. "Mind your own business. I can't afford to lose scholarship money, like some people."

"What's that supposed to mean?" I demanded.

"Nothing." She fell on the bed.

"I get overwhelmed before exams, too. I understand the pressure."

"Just let me deal with this, okay?" My friend popped in her earbuds and turned over in bed. Erika overdosed during our last year before earning our bachelor's degree together, as we planned.

"Marsha, it's fine. I'm glad you're okay." A truck hauling wooden pallets jumped in front of her on the highway. It hit a bump, and one of the pallets flew out of the back and under her car. She had no time to react, running over it and catching a flat.

"I tried to avoid, but I couldn't." Marsha's voice shook. "Roadside assistance said someone will come in another hour or two."

"Do you need me to come and get you?" I offered, sensing her panic.

"No, no, I'm fine, Ms. Chelsea."

"How many times have you called me that, and I always say Chelsea is fine? You're practically family. Call me Chell."

She laughed at the idea. "I know. I just do it out of respect and am so grateful for this job."

Marsha came to Haven about three years ago. After working part-time for a year, she applied for her current full-time position, earning her spot and replacing my previous executive assistant and center manager. I didn't doubt my decision to hire Marsha and couldn't ask for someone more dependable and trustworthy.

"Why don't you take the rest of the day off," I suggested. "I can manage."

"I don't want to inconvenience you."

"Your safety is not an inconvenience. I insist," I said more firmly. "Get an early start on your weekend. Whatever you need to do here can wait until you get back."

Marsha had plans to go out of town this weekend. After I got Marsha to understand that the place wouldn't fall apart if she missed one afternoon, I returned to shredding old files. I heard a message notification on my cell. Charla apologized for missing my call and said she would talk soon.

The sound of my stomach growling meant I reached a stopping point with the paperwork. Running on only a banana and graham cracker, I craved chicken shawarma pasta from a nearby Greek café. I grabbed my purse and locked up the office.

I rushed inside the Greek and Lebanese café, smiling as I stood in the short line, happy to beat the lunch crowd. I placed my order and sat at a table by the large window. I looked around, trying to pass the time, and took out my cell phone. I saw a tweet from one of the local news stations. A park maintenance worker found a dead woman. I opened it and started to read the article. My head began to tingle when I saw the face of the dead woman, Brienne Landrieu, one of Haven's former residents.

The teenage-looking hostess walked over with my lunch tied up in a bag. I still held the cell phone, but the screen had gone dark. I couldn't finish the article after reading the name and seeing the image they used. I felt uneasy when I stood up and put my hand on the table to catch my balance. The hostess checked on me. I nodded and took a sip of the iced cold Lebanese tea that I always get with honey. I walked out of the restaurant, still feeling anxious about Brienne. I walked past my car. Realizing what I had done, I took a few steps back, opened the door to my white BMW, and tried my sister again.

"Come on, pick up," I pleaded into the phone.

"Hey, Chell, I'm so sorry. I got caught up with this monthly report."

"Someone found Brienne dead in the park this morning." The words flew out, crashing the conversation.

"Wait, what?" Then, a pause on my sister's end.

"Brienne, a past resident at Haven."

"Oh, her!" Charla started to digest the information. "That is awful."

Charla, a Haven board member, donated and volunteered. One night, we ran into Brienne while dining at a restaurant. I didn't make an introduction, hesitant about the woman's privacy, but Brienne introduced herself to my sister and explained how we knew each other. She had a second job working evening shifts, saving up to buy a house. Hearing her talk that night about her goals made me proud.

"Wasn't she threatened?" Charla asked.

Brienne stressed about the recovery process and started to show signs of depression. I worried she might relapse, so I asked her to meet in private. She said that an influential person from her past had threatened her recently, but she didn't reveal who or give details about the threat. I confided in Charla after I spoke with the troubled woman.

"Yes."

"Did she ever say by who?"

"No, she didn't." I thought it over. "Now, I wished she had. Maybe if I had pressed her more."

"You can't control that, Chell. So, what happened?"

"The article didn't say much besides that a maintenance worker called 911 saying he found a dead woman in the park. They suspect an overdose. The reporter wrote that Brienne's car was in the parking lot, and her body sat up against a tree. They are waiting for an update from the police department but encouraged anyone with information to contact them."

"Oh my God!" Charla's tone rose.

"I know." My voice cracked.

"Chell, where are you?"

"I just picked up lunch, and I'm about to head back to work."

"Just take a minute to calm down before you drive off."

"I'm good." I didn't believe my own words. I appreciated my sister's concern, but her motherly instructions were slightly annoying.

"Let me know if you need me, okay?"

"Yeah, okay."

When I returned to Haven, I heard voices from the dining area. The cafeteria workers plopped large scoops of chicken alfredo pasta onto plates. I rushed toward the administrative side of the building. I didn't want anyone to ask me about Brienne. My cell vibrated. It was Marsha. She knew.

"This is so awful." Marsha began.

"I know. I can't wrap my head around it."

"I'm not that surprised, though."

"What do you mean?" I asked, shocked by her comment.

"I don't mean it like that; it's just, you know, her lifestyle. Girls who make money so easily often get into trouble." Marsha preached.

It's not a secret that Brienne had a shady past, but most people at Haven did. I admired her efforts to change. Brienne made reckless decisions, but I never held it against her or anyone else who sought recovery. I advised the staff to do the same. "Yes, but she changed." I defended. "Everyone, especially those who come here, has a past."

"I'm just saying that I know the kind of person she was and where that life can lead."

I wondered what all Marsha knew. "Okay, I understand, but you know that we advocate for people like her."

"Yes, you're right." Marsha conceded, her stance unwilling to hold up her opinion.

"I don't mean to get defensive, but she is one of our success stories."

"I know." Marsha agreed.

CHAPTER 4

CHAD

I tilted my head, lifting the bottom of the water bottle to the sun and squirting more ice water into my mouth. I needed to catch my breath after my routine morning run. The damp ground from the morning drizzle muddied my running shoes. I parked my car curbside on the exterior side of the park, closer to the university. I took out my backup pair from the trunk to change into. Thick yellow caution tape wrapped around the parking lot, restrooms, and nearby trees. A forensics team and police officers tracked back and forth through the sectioned area. They examined the base of a tree. The hoodie of my jogging suit concealed my face, but I noticed one of them get up from a squatting position with an object in their hand and look my way, his stare lingering for a few seconds too long. I got in my car and drove off.

I have always watched people. When I was a kid, my mother, Yvette Celestine, let me go to the community park, usually on my own, except when she trolled. She talked to her friends about the fine single men who took their kids to the park. During the summer, the community center pool opened, and Yvette would stroll through with cut-off denim shorts, a crop top, and extensions half up and half down. She played the mother role, pointing with her long American tip nails and shouting for me not to go in the deep end. One summer, I swam out too far, and she ran to the other end of the pool, screaming for someone else to jump in and save me. An older kid lifted me out of the water and sat me poolside. Yvette wiped me down with a towel, saying something about just getting her weave put in and how much the hair cost.

The other kids came with their parents, but their mom and dad played with them in the water and helped if they got scared. I admired the fathers that held their children above water, teaching them how to swim. I maneuvered through them, keeping my distance. I didn't want to get hit by little flailing arms and legs. Yvette would sit in a poolside chair flipping through VIBE magazine, scanning the pool with her man radar.

One time in late summer, right before I returned to school, I watched her slip a magazine into the water, shoving it away so it started to drift before she cried out for someone to save it. She targeted a tall, muscular, dark-skinned black man exiting the pool with his daughter. He turned to go back for it and handed the dripping pages to my mother. She started a conversation, and he motioned to the little toddler next to him, introducing his child. Yvette didn't look my way or attempt an introduction. She slipped him a piece of paper. He smiled and returned to the little girl who refused to remove her arm floaties, whining because her pool time ended.

That Fall, I started third grade and learned to write in cursive. I practiced every day when I got home. I liked how I could connect the letters. Each week, my teacher, Mrs. Dauphine, would pick a student's writing assignment to show as a model for the class. One Friday, she chose my cursive passage. It was a half school day, and I was eager to get home. I rushed off the bus to the apartment to show off my work. I don't know why, but my mother never took an interest. If the police didn't show up at her door and teachers didn't call, Yvette was doing her job. I heard her voice coming from the bedroom. I listened to her high-pitched vocals from the back of the apartment, not caring if I disturbed her gossip session. I rushed in to show her the gold star on my paper.

My mother was on top of a man, laughing and screaming, dookie braids swinging. Handcuffs hung from the edge of the bed. I glanced away to focus on anything else in the room and noticed a police uniform in a pile on the floor.

Yvette grabbed the sheets to cover her body while the man quickly turned his face away. I recognized the guy with the little girl from the pool. "Why aren't you in school?" Her weak attempt at chastising. "What did I tell you bout comin' in my room like that?!" Her flaming eyes burned a hole through my paper. "Close my damn door!"

I ran out of her bedroom and down the short hallway into my room, slamming the door behind me. I threw my writing in the trash and my book sack on the bed, burying my head in the secondhand Chicago Bulls comforter, and cried. Yvette came storming in, yanking me by the arm off the bed and slapping me across the face. I spoiled her chance with the man from the pool. After she left, I walked over to the TV and popped in one of the VCR tapes I used to record some of my favorite shows. I sat on the bed and watched Zack transform into the black

Power Ranger to fight the evil villains. I thought about how fun it would be to wear a suit and hide my identity. I could be anyone I wanted, and no one would know.

I hated drivers who made it a point to examine your car while waiting for the traffic light to turn green. One day, I want to ask one of them if they're taking inventory or just want to know how much and what year. I needed to get home and clean up. I stifled a yawn and wiped my tired eyes. My legs ached from my run, and my stomach growled. I wanted some comfort food.

I had been living in Lafayette for a while and had grown accustomed to various food choices and festivals. They loved to eat, and the list of dining spots proved it. This city would have me packing on an extra fifty if I didn't keep up with my running routine. Back home, I had my share of good meals. Yvette was a lot of things, but she knew how to cook when she wanted. Big meals were usually centered around impressing a man or special occasions, like birthdays.

I settled on a breakfast combo from a local place on the north side. I called my order in to save time. The popular morning spot would have a list of orders ahead of me if I waited too long.

The girl at the counter, her hair still wrapped from last night, hurried to hand me a to-go box when I first arrived, smiling, looking me up and down before turning around to face the kitchen to give me a back view. Ignoring her performance, I checked my box and saw pancakes with eggs and bacon instead of the hamburger patty, eggs, grits, and biscuits. I didn't have time for this. She returned the container and swiveled her head around to tell the cooks in the back. Twenty minutes later, I got up to approach the counter again. The former friendly employee leaned against a wall, giving me sideways glances as she chatted with patrons eating at a table. The line stretched to the door. The manager greeted me with a fresh box and opened it so I could inspect my order. It contained an extra patty. I nodded my thanks and toted the hefty breakfast to the door. "Come back and see us," the manager called out. I slid my shades back on to face the morning light, ready to face the long day.

CHAPTER 5

CHARLA

I sat at my home office desk early that evening with my camera on. I watched the number of participants joining the Zoom call increase to twice the average attendance. Dede was at her father's house, so I didn't have to worry about my curious child popping up on the screen as she peeked from the doorway. Seeing the faces of those who are usually too busy to attend regular sessions and show up for news like this amazed me. The next scheduled meeting wasn't for a few more weeks, but after the death of one of Haven's former residents made headlines, my sister addressed questions to the group. A few board members also raised concerns when they heard the police contacted Chelsea about Brienne's connection to the organization.

"Thank you all for being here. I would like to call this meeting to order. The time is 5:30 PM." Chelsea smiled from the table of a meeting room at the center. Her assistant, Marsha, sat off to the side, opened her laptop, and took minutes. Our meetings switched to Zoom during the COVID shutdown, and we kept it that way ever since. My sister smiled as she took in all the participants' screens. "I know this meeting is short notice, but as you all know, we recently lost one of our past clients." She gathered her thoughts for a moment. "Brienne Landrieu will be missed. She had a bright future, but her life was taken too soon." Solemn nods harmoniously played across the screens. Marsha took a break from typing. A couple of these nodding heads joined the board after Brienne left but joined in the camaraderie of the virtual mourning. "I know there have been legitimate concerns about the police coming to the center. I want all of you to know that the officer informed me it is just routine protocol, and they are checking all leads."

"Excuse me, Chelsea, but how did the police find out Brienne was at Haven?" A veteran board member, Jocelyn Francis, didn't like her time being wasted. She ran a few businesses and owned multiple properties in the city. Mrs. Francis reached for a notepad and pen as we got to the first point on the agenda.

"The identities of Haven's clients are private, just like any other recovery program," Chelsea explained. "This situation is different. Someone submitted a video to the police showing Brienne talking about our services. It was a promotional spot for her church." My sister glanced down at the paperwork in front of her. "As you can see from our financial records, Greater Living is one of Haven's major donors."

"I see." Mrs. Francis sat back, tapping her pen on the notepad.

"Is Haven being linked to her death, or is this a general line of questioning to confirm her participation in the program?" Leslie Harper, the marketing and public relations representative and local socialite, turned on her screen. A quick camera change from her polished profile picture to the made-up woman seated in front of an array of hanging bookshelves that held the year's must-reads and ornamental décor that hung in between.

"I hope not. I don't think so." Chelsea shook her head, batting away the idea. "She had left by the time the program aired."

"I know, but since she did this promo about Haven and-" she cleared her throat. "Excuse me if this seems insensitive. Now that she's found dead, it could speak ill about the program." The PR expert went on to clarify. "That connection could deter our current supporters and hurt our chances to secure new ones." From the look on my sister's face, I see that her priority wasn't about the center's image but about helping to find out what happened to Brienne. I moved my finger to unmute my microphone, but my little sister beat me.

"Of course, we must keep the center's reputation in mind," Chelsea's edgy tone escalated, "but we must help in any way we can find out what happened. The police didn't confirm that this was drug-related. There could be foul play." My sister took a deep breath. "Our support would show that Haven still cares about their clients even after they exit the program."

"I agree with you completely, Chelsea. That is in Haven's best interest." A recent addition to the board, Damien Brown, sat in an office with a minimalist touch, a prominent piece of contemporary art hung on the wall above his head. The cashmere Brunello Cucinelli blazer and open-collared shirt complimented his brown complexion and dark black hair.

"Yes, of course it would." Leslie emphatically agreed earning a smile from Damien. "I'm just suggesting that we prepare."

We proceeded to discuss what our statement should say. Most agreed that Haven should express condolences and show that we would help the authorities in any way we can but clarify that the center is not connected to her death. We didn't know the details of Brienne Landrieu's relations outside the organization. Leslie would draft something to send to all those on the call for review.

We finally moved on to other topics. My legs grew restless, ready to jump out of my chair. Marsha spoke about the annual Community Hearts Charity event. A local venue invited charities to set up every year for an upscale setting where attendees could enjoy gourmet cuisine, wine, cocktails, and tote glamorous and tasty giveaways. Vendors went above and beyond decorating their stations according to the chosen theme. Chelsea talked my ear off for days as she racked up on vintage fall décor and romantic art pieces from specialty boutiques to match this year's theme, Fall in Love with Giving.

"Attendance increased this year compared to last." Marsha spoke cheerfully. "Most attendees donated using the QR code I put on the table, but some still gave me a check or cash."

"How much did you collect?" I handled Haven's online donations and budget when allocating funds, but Chelsea's executive assistant collected donations given at events or mailed to the office. Compared to the current tech-savvy ways to donate via app or online, some older donors still prefer antiquated ways of giving. Marsha kept those gifts secured until her scheduled trip to the bank to make a deposit. Some people requested a confirmation after they donated. Marsha emailed me a report with contact information for each donor and the amount they gave. I haven't received one for this event yet.

"About $800 in cash and $1,000 in checks."

"Okay, thanks. Will you send a report soon?"

"Yes, of course. I guess I forgot," Marsha said nervously, "with everything going on."

"Yes, I understand. Send it when you have a minute." I excused her delay in reporting.

Marsha finished her recap of the charity event, signaling that I should give the financial report.

After I gave the board Haven's financial status, including the figures Marsha gave and our budget for the remainder of the year, I switched my camera off and turned up the volume on my laptop. I went into the kitchen to grab some water and a snack. When I sat back in my chair, the board bounced around ideas about hosting a fundraiser to bring in additional funds.

"We could use the money," said one of them.

"Is this a good time to host a fundraiser?" asked another.

"Maybe we should revisit this after things have settled." Leslie chimed in.

The direction of the meeting and the idea of distancing the recovery program from one of its residents turned my sister off. I sent her a text message to say we could chat later.

"Chelsea, can you hang on a minute after the meeting?" Khristian Babineaux, one of Haven's counselors and a reliable meeting attendee, came off mute. He was closer to Chelsea's age but acted much older. Khristian kept a buzz cut, nearly bald, and opted for the shirt and tie under the knit sweater look. He seemed controlling, not one who played well with others and preferred his ideas. He had been reticent for the duration of the meeting. He kept rearranging items on his desk during certain parts of the discussion. Mr. Babineaux always had an opinion about matters involving the center. This evening, he only expressed condolences for the deceased and a couple of nods during commentary.

"Sure. Just call my cell when we're done." My sister concluded the meeting.

I got a notification from Travis. He'd seen the story on the news. I called him back after I shut down my laptop.

"Hey, I just wanted to see how things are going."

"I'm fine; Chell is the one taking some heat."

"Yeah, I figured."

"I think it will slow down soon, though. Linking Brienne's death to the center is absurd to me."

"Right, how did that happen?"

"Someone at her church sent a promo video about Haven that she did. I don't know if they thought it would help the case."

"You never know. That's wild."

"Yeah, it is."

"You know I'm here if you need anything."

"Thanks, I appreciate that because I know you mean it." Travis was there through my divorce from Justin.

"Of course."

CHAPTER 6

CHELSEA

I lay on my living room sofa with my cell on my stomach; the speaker turned up. I let out a long exhale, thinking about the board meeting. I reached for a handful of hot popcorn and melted chocolate in the large glass bowl. I let the Roku home screen play, ready to stream something suspenseful after I hung up with Khristian.

"So, what's up? I hope there aren't any other fires we need to put out."

His voice strained as he greeted me, unsure of how to respond. "Brienne and I have history."

"What?" I sat up, almost knocking my phone on the floor, shocked by this admission. Khristian started working as a center counselor before Brienne arrived. I remember he turned down counseling her because of his workload. I didn't know about any other connection they had. "You never said this before."

"I know, and I apologize for that. When I saw Brienne's name on the client paperwork, I reached out to let her know I worked there, but she was fine with it and said we could keep it private."

"How do you know her?" I wanted to know how deep their relations went.

"We dated for a little while."

"How long ago?

"Long before my time at Haven."

"Okay, so why are you telling me now?" I waited to hear how it related to her death. I never saw him as violent. Now, I feared how far this confession would go.

"The police contacted me." He blurted, sniffling.

"They've been interviewing everyone from the center." Officer Champagne and another cop made this clear when they met with staff.

"I know, but this whole thing has been on my mind since she died." The sniffles stopped, and he started to chuckle. "Sorry." He paused. "She's not the person you thought she was."

"Oh?" Brienne wasn't as well-liked as I thought.

"The main reason we stopped talking is because once she found out something about a person, she used it against them."

"What do you mean? Like what?"

"Things that could hurt a person. Brienne didn't mind making enemies. She was always like that, even back in college."

"Did she do that to you?" I questioned.

"Uhm, hmm." His admission slipped between tight lips that fought to reveal more than his comfort level allowed.

"I see." I wondered what Brienne had on him.

"I don't know what happened to her. Like I said to the cop, we didn't really speak anymore." Khristian piped up.

"I appreciate you telling me, and I think you should tell the police everything you know.

"I will."

"I wish I would have known about this before."

"I understand how you feel, and once again, I apologize, but please know that I kept it professional."

"I trust that you did." My phone alerted me to an incoming call from my mother. I ended the call with Khristian and snacked on another handful of salty and sweet. I went into the kitchen to get some iced water. I need a breather before speaking to anyone else. The screensaver danced across my flatscreen. My suspenseful escape would have to wait.

I sat on my mother's cream sofa, moving my sister's jacket and purse. I put the rust-colored throw pillow on my lap. Our mother invited us over for dinner. I suspected she had spoken to Charla about the board meeting. I looked at the dark wooden table in the corner of the living room. It used to have a framed picture of my mother and father. I couldn't remember the last time I saw a picture of my dad in the house. That season of our lives was long ago, and we rarely spoke of it. A bouquet adorned the table with smaller pictures of me and my sister in grade school. I thought about what Khristian said and Marsha's comment about Brienne's background. I knew Brienne hadn't told me everything about her past, but I wondered which omission led to her death.

"It'll be ready in a little bit." Our mother called out from the kitchen before placing a lid back on one of the pots, leaving a small opening as she'd always done to let the steam escape. She went into the dining room to set the table. My sister and I got up to help, but she waved us back down. "I'm fine. Y'all just relax and hang out." She moved about the dining room and then on to another room, a busybody who rejected the luxury of sitting down. Helena Richard kept a clean house, and no amount of cooking she did would make her kitchen an exception. The pristine marble countertops matched the cabinets and drawers illuminated by metallic handles and appliances.

My sister got up and went into the kitchen. I could hear the clinking of a glass and the soft thud of a bottle landing on marble.

"Be careful with that wine bottle on my countertop." Our mother scolded, eyeing Charla while she poured.

I started scrolling through my social feed, looking for something to fill the headspace that the board meeting cracked open. I grew tired of it quickly, my mind not grasping the moving images and captions that slipped under my fingertip. I felt a wave of body heat coming from behind and the slight move of a hand across stiff fabric. I whipped my head around to aim back at my sister's nosey stare as she stood behind the spotless couch, bravely holding the glass of wine. She stalked my social media page from above.

"Would you have a seat, please?" I begged, rolling my eyes.

Charla reluctantly moved over to the adjacent rust-colored chair, sitting upright and leaning towards me with her legs crossed and glass dangling over her knee. "Did they post anything yet?" Tonight, my sister's ex celebrated his youngest daughter's fourth birthday. Justin Hill had remarried, and Delilah was with her father, stepmom, and half-sister. Charla's edginess wasn't because of his new wife or second child; she'd moved on. My sister hated being without Dede.

"Why don't you look for yourself?"

"I don't follow him," she snared, taking a sip. "You do." She resented the idea that I remained social media friends with her ex.

"He's my niece's father, and he's still like family." A don't go there stare from Charla. Justin and Charla met in middle school, so their long-time relationship earned him a seat at our family table long before they made it official.

"Okay, whatever. Would you please just do it?" She snapped.

I made a move to put down my phone. "I just want to know what Dede is doing," her tone didn't have as much sting, "and you have access to that."

I clicked to pull up Justin's page, feeling like a stalker. He recently posted a picture of his youngest daughter, Bailey, sitting at a table in front of a glitzy multilayered cake. The toddler's excited eyes focused on the giant elephant on top, centered by a vintage carousel pole draped in silver, gold, and pink beads, with a jewel embedded in the center of the circus animal's forehead. Matching gems of the same size outlined the top and bottom of the decadent art piece. Dede sat beside her stepsister and smiled, with Justin, his wife Lorraine, and their parents standing in a neat row behind them. "He just posted a couple of pictures," I reported. I summarized the cover photo, turning my phone screen so my neurotic sister could see. I held the phone out long enough for her to peek.

"Did they get the cake from a jewelry store?" She mocked. "I mean, the girl is four."

"I think it's exquisite, with a touch of childhood."

"A touch is right. What else?" She reminded me that I said he posted more than one.

Past annoyed, I swiped to the next photo. Bailey was seated on a sofa, her birthday outfit more visible. It was a soft pink and brown two-piece top and leggings paired with cheetah-printed flats. She placed her hands in her lap and flashed a broad smile, this time aimed straight at the camera, surrounded by gifts. "Aww, so you got her the kitchen set?" I zoomed in on the pink farmhouse play kitchen with chalkboard, storage shelves, and accessories. "It's so cute. Didn't we both have one of these growing up?"

"You sure did." My mother crept back into the living room. "Just about begged for it." She'd left us to troll online but still tuned in to the conversation.

"I figured it was age-appropriate." Charla nodded into her glass.

"I think it's great that you did that." I closed the social media app and shut my screen off. "A mature move."

"I couldn't have my daughter show up empty-handed. She wanted something for her little sister, so I shopped with her online." Charla shrugged, finishing up her wine.

"Let's eat," our mother motioned to the dining area.

We filled our stomachs with the comforts of perfectly seasoned smothered chicken and potatoes over jasmine rice and a hearty portion of buttered green beans on the side. Our mom loved how the jasmine made her kitchen smell, claiming it tasted better than plain white rice.

"So, how was the meeting?" My mother asked, aiming it more at me than Charla.

"It was as can be expected," I replied between bites. "The board wants to take the business route, and I get that." Charla shifted in her seat, glancing at our mother.

"Do you agree with that approach?" Helena dug, displaying a warm smile while holding the shovel.

"It is what it is. We do need to think about the organization's reputation. It will be affected by how we handle the personal angle." A supporting nod from my mother and Charla. I didn't need them to agree just to appease me. "I'm sure Charla feels differently."

"Actually," Charla finished chewing her last bits of food, "I agree with both angles." She kept her focus on me. "Haven is a business and should operate like one if you want the respect of your board and donors. The organization deals with the deep struggles of the individuals it helps, so you can't escape that aspect, and we shouldn't. Haven's brand depends on how you and your staff care for the people who turn to you for help."

"I appreciate that. I wish the rest of the board would have heard it." I reminded my sister how quiet she had been on the call today.

"I think you spoke on that matter just fine." Charla sat up straighter, going into defense mode. "I followed your orders to let you hold your title and run the meetings." It was true that in the past, I asked her not to be so aggressive in meetings. Charla likes to help, but her version is more like taking over.

"Yeah, fine." I moved my empty plate to the side.

"Well," our mother filled the space, "a healthy debate is good for the soul. Just don't let it escalate to more than that." She attempted to ease the tension. "The news report was heartbreaking. The public will see that your organization helped this young woman to get as far as she did."

"I think so, too." Charla agreed.

"So do I."

"Any dessert?" Our mother immediately stood up and went to the kitchen to open the refrigerator, retrieving a bowl of banana pudding. Helena knew how to change the topic when necessary. We were on our way to lighter conversations and sweet tooth satisfaction.

CHAPTER 7

CHAD

The evening grew dark as I sat in my car a safe distance from the stately house with its manicured lawn, lined flowerbeds, and trained trees framing the property, careful not to steal attention from the home. The three women exited the home, one after the other, chatting about things people in neighborhoods like this talk about. I wanted to hear what carried the conversation, what made them laugh, snicker, or indifferent. They had been in the house for hours. My legs stiffened for the second time.

The older woman, Helena, their mother, was tall, and her past middle-aged body settled in but still in shape. Her neat hair bun rested high on her head, and her dry-cleaned pantsuit was a bit over-dressed for dinner with your children. The older sister, Charla, wore skinny jeans with a camel-tone top. She stood slightly shorter than Helena. Her rich, dark brown, straight-edged bob rested above a crisp collar. She had curves, but not as thick as the younger sister, Chelsea. Her voluptuous frame sported an above-the-knee burnt orange sweater dress with booties. Her long, thick natural coils roamed free about her head and down the front of her face.

The elder sibling suddenly turned her head in my direction. I pulled my cap down and dug into the plastic bag on the passenger seat. I packed food containers and put a delivery device on the dashboard if anyone questioned my presence. When the heat of her stare started to cool, I looked back at the house. The mother stood in the opened doorway, waving her daughters off as they got in their vehicles.

JUNE 1995

I heard a knock at the door. I grabbed a chair to see who it was. A head of clean-shaven coils blocked the peephole. My mother warned me not to open the door for anyone when she wasn't home. She'd just started another job. I jumped off the chair and put it back in the kitchen. I went to the window in the living room and carefully pulled the blind down just enough to see the parking lot. I saw an SUV that I didn't recognize. There was another knock; this time, the person pounded harder and announced who he was. I opened the door and saw the man Yvette called my father.

His dark brown skin, clean-shaven appearance, and how he tucked his shirt in his pants reminded me of the father on Family Matters. My father was taller, with less weight and more hair. I stayed by the door after he stepped into the living room. I remember when he popped up one summer when Yvette took me to the beach. We'd been there for hours and started packing up to leave. My mother yelled something about us not being worth his time. He looked tired, and his clothes were covered in sand as if he had been there all day. He didn't spend the day with us, though.

My father walked around the apartment, inspecting, turning his nose up, and sucking air between his teeth as he looked about. His eyes lingered on the shelf in the living room where Yvette kept her dolls. One shelf held what she called our royal African ancestors. A bare-chested king wore a crown and necklace with a blue and red bird spreading its gold wings. He had a wrap around his waist that hung down to his ankles. His queen sat straight on a throne, layers of gold bands going up her neck and braids pinned under a high gold crown. She wore a white and gold dress, holding a baby wrapped in purple and gold linen. A Native American family was on the lower shelf. The father had a spear and wore a feathered headpiece that framed his body to his shoes. The mother sat upright on a woven pillow in a tribal dress. Her hair parted down the middle in two long, thick braids. A little boy and girl wore bold-colored patterns and sat peacefully beside her. Yvette always told people we had Indian in the family, even when they didn't ask.

My father's eyes moved over to the kitchen counter. "Is this your dinner?" He glanced at the half-made bologna sandwich. I nodded. I'd left the loaf of bread and meat pack beside the paper plate. "No mayo or cheese?"

Yvette hadn't received her paycheck yet, so groceries were slim, but she wouldn't want me to tell him that. "No, sometimes I like it plain."

He smirked, looking me up and down. "What time is your mother coming back?"

I shrugged. "A couple of hours, I guess. She's at work."

He stopped himself from laughing. "You want some real food?"

I jerked my head at the offer before looking back at the dry sandwich on the counter. "Yes!"

"Let's go." He swung the door open. I snatched my Power Rangers keychain off the hook and followed him out the door, locking up before running toward the stairs.

The SUV had that new car smell. I slid into the clean and shiny seat. The black carpets were dust-free. Once strapped in, I didn't move from my spot in the backseat. "How does a burger, fries, and a milkshake sound?" My father's dark eyes examined me in the rearview mirror.

"Sounds good." I wanted to smile but held it in. Yvette told me to stop being soft. I hadn't had a treat like that in a long time. My mother rarely took us out, saying it was a waste of money when we had food at home. She didn't mind when men took her out to eat.

We went through the drive-thru, and my father pulled into a parking spot near the restaurant. I heard the click of the doors unlocking. He grabbed my food bag and shake. He ordered a soda and fries for himself. I took off my seatbelt and opened the door before jumping down. It was best that we ate outside because I feared making a stain. We sat at a nearby table covered by a green umbrella. He laid out my food before sipping his drink and eating the fries. "Go on now, eat," he commanded. I tore into the juicy cheeseburger and steak fries, chasing it with the sweet vanilla shake. "Slow down," he chuckled. "Your food isn't going anywhere. We have time." I kicked my legs back and forth under the table as I sipped more of the frozen treat, slower this time. A smile escaped between bites of bread, meat, and melted cheese. I enjoyed eating with my father. It felt different compared to being with my mother.

On the way back to the apartment, I prayed I didn't mix up the time Yvette told me she would get off. I didn't want her to know about the time I shared with my father. Given the chance, she would crush this moment between her spiky claws before dropping it in the trash among the other debris she wanted out of the apartment.

I spotted the late 1980s Toyota Camry as my father approached the apartment building. I hung my head as the knot in my stomach formed. "I'll handle it," he said before we exited the SUV.

"Where have you been?" My mother demanded from the doorway. I was about to respond when my father stopped me. He walked up to my mother, meeting her at eye level.

"I took my son to get some real food." His voice boomed through the doorway, forcing my mother to take a few steps back into the apartment to let us inside. He closed the door.

Yvette grabbed me by the shirt; her fingers gripped the large, washed-out letter M. "Don't ever take my son out of my home without my permission!" She fired at my father.

"Maybe if you kept decent food here, I wouldn't need to." He forced her to release me. "What are you doing with the money I send?"

"That shit you call support is nothin' to brag about. It barely covers the rent."

"The rent can't be that much." He looked around the apartment like he did when he first arrived.

"Whateva!" Yvette rolled her head around. "You plan to pay for somethin' better?" He didn't respond. "Thought not."

He took a slip of paper out of his pocket and handed it to me. "Call me if you need something." I reached for it, but Yvette snatched it from my hand and ripped it up, letting the pieces fall to the floor.

"I take care of his needs. You have a family to provide for, remember?" Her words sliced through the apartment's stale air. I slipped into the hallway near my bedroom, leaning against the wall.

"I will always provide for my son." His tone lost some of its bass; he had run out of steam.

"Yeah, okay." Yvette sensed she had the upper hand. "Keep sending your lil' check if you want to." She moved towards him to get him to leave.

He didn't budge; instead, he stood up straighter, ready for war. "Don't disrespect me in front of my son."

"You need to respect me in my home." She braced up to him, getting in his face.

I felt the urge to jump in and stop them, but my legs felt numb. I turned away as I slid down to the floor. I heard shuffling before the crashing sound of the lamp hitting the floor and the front door swinging open before slamming shut. They fell quiet before I heard my mother sniffling. She called out to me. "Get me a broom." My legs felt tingly as the feeling started to come back. I retrieved it from the side of the refrigerator. I handed her the broom. She was hunched over, scanning the floor, picking up the larger broken ceramic pieces. "I'm about to boil some sausage and macaroni tonight. Go get cleaned up."

I stuttered to get the words out. "I already ate-"

"You will eat what I cook!" Yvette snapped her neck up at me, hot, misty eyes daring me to say another word.

CHAPTER 8

OCTOBER 2023

CHARLA

I sat in the driver's seat, texting Travis. He told me my ex's wife was jealous of me back when we were in high school, but I didn't believe it. I parked in the quiet neighborhood near their community park and a pond.

I'm picking up Dede.

Praying for you. *lol*

Delilah bounced down the driveway, her curly ponytail carving a trail of soft circles in the wind. Her father exited the front door shortly after, carrying her weekend bag and a stuffed animal I'd never seen before. My ex-husband's toned arms and trim waistline said he kept his gym membership active. His previous thick crop of hair, which he wore higher on the top and shaved in the back, had grown into shoulder-length locs, a style I never imagined him in. His wife, Lorraine, was very skinny, approaching frail. She was hot on his trail, turning towards the mailbox and retrieving a few envelopes. The three of us graduated from the same high school. Lorraine and I were never what you would call friends, but our circles crossed. I was a Beta and National Honor Society member and served as student body president for the last two years in high school. Lorraine did well academically but was more concerned with securing her financial future through a pro-athlete or millionaire tech nerd. I don't know how she ended up with Justin. He worked in IT for the state and consulted on the side.

I hugged and kissed Dede before lifting her into the backseat. Justin opened the opposite backdoor, put her bag on the seat, and placed a smiling, fluffy tiger on top. We greeted each other in the routine cordial manner we perfected over the years before I hopped back in the front seat and started the engine. The tap on my window made me jump, and I let out a slight cry as my leg hit the knee bolster. Justin stood up against the door. Dede stuck her head between the front seats, asking if I was okay. "Yes, Nugget." I rolled the window down.

"Sorry, I didn't mean to startle you," Justin apologized. He put his hands in his pockets before taking them out again and pressing them against the door.

"I'm fine. Is everything okay?" Back at the house, his wife lingered at the end of the drive, shuffling through the same three letters. Our marriage dissolved when Dede was three. We were both willing to co-parent for Dede's sake. Justin could never meet me to exchange our daughter without Lorraine being nearby. She was a silhouette waiting on the passenger side or a stick figure pacing back and forth in the distance.

"Yeah, it's fine. Uhm, Dede asked about Bailey coming with her to go places with you sometimes." He struggled to speak.

"Oh, she did?" I wondered what put that in my daughter's head. She had never asked it before. Behind us, Delilah played with the tiger. "Are y'all okay with that?"

"Yeah, I'm okay with it."

"Well, I don't know about that." His daughter didn't know me, and I felt she shouldn't be in my care. "We can discuss it later." I planned to express my true feelings away from the eager ears of my daughter. "What about-?" I nodded towards his wife, who was now halfway up the driveway, pulling weeds.

Justin leaned in the window, lowering his tone. "We discussed it, and I told her I don't see a problem."

"I see." I knew that conversation didn't go over as easily as he delivered. He wouldn't dare go against her because Lorraine ran the operations of that household. She would never release Bailey to me. My ex lost something when he got into that relationship. He seemed weaker, less sure, not the confident, ambitious, most likely-to-succeed young black male I remembered.

"Well, think about it, and let me know." He backed away from the window, Lorraine now at the front door, her body language urging him to hurry up.

"Okay, I'll get back to you."

"Bye, sweetie." He blew a kiss to Dede, and she cheerfully returned it.

We said our goodbyes, and I waved at Lorraine. She did the same.

I drove away from the smothering confines of the cookie-cutter houses. I asked Dede about her visit. My daughter went into reporter mode.

"The birthday party was really fun." She gave a breakdown of who gave what gifts. "Bailey loved the kitchen set we bought her!" Her voice escalated. "We went to the park, and I helped her on the monkey bars and pushed her on the swing." Then Dede got to the part I wanted to hear about. "On the way back from a store, we were all in the car, and I asked if Bailey could come to the museum with us."

"That was sweet of you to ask." I couldn't be the one to break my daughter's heart with the hammer of reality.

"Daddy said it was a good idea when I asked about it." Justin knew it wasn't. "But Mrs. Lorraine made a face."

"Oh, she did?" I could count on Dede to give me the real story.

"Yeah, I saw her in the car mirror." My daughter tried to imitate her stepmom. I stifled a laugh at her childlike impression.

"So, you don't think she liked the idea?" I shamelessly pried for more information.

"I don't think so. Daddy said they would talk about it, and then Mrs. Lorraine hit his leg."

"Wait." I slammed the brakes, throwing us forward, almost running a stop sign. "She hit him?" I stressed for clarity.

"On the leg." She motioned. "The way you do when we're in church, and I'm moving around a lot, making too much noise."

"Oh, that. Okay."

"Daddy didn't like it, though." She frowned. "I wasn't trying to cause any trouble."

"No, of course not. I'm sure everything is fine." I tried to reassure her.

"Okay." She thought a moment. "I just thought my little sister could be with us and Mr. Preston sometimes, like I go with them."

"Did you discuss Mr. Preston with your father and his wife?" I questioned.

"No, ma'am." She said confidently. "I remember our talk." She quoted the air.

"Okay, good," I explained to her that I didn't want her talking about Mommy's friends at Daddy's house. If I married again, her father would find out from me. Dede never met most of the men I dated. Preston and I started dating a little over four months ago, and recently, he ran into us on a frozen yogurt run. "Well, your grandmother baked some pumpkin spice cookies." Dede tossed the tiger in the air. "I want one!" She forgot all about her proposed excursion.

CHAPTER 9

CHELSEA

I hate Mondays like the next person, but today felt heavier than most. Repeating the polished statement from Haven to reporters was draining, but thankfully, by the afternoon, it had slowed down. I left a little early, leaving Marsha at the center. I was trapped in my office since seven this morning. My assistant was kind enough to pop out and grab us both lunches; otherwise, I would still be running on orange juice and a half-eaten biscuit. I was going to meet one of our board members, Damien Brown. A few months ago, he contacted me at the center. He testified about being connected to our mission and wanting to serve in a volunteer capacity. I was impressed when I met him for the first time. I imagined his social media feed filled with collaborative pictures of the upper-class parish society and the top 40 under 40, but his page was bare, besides commentary posts. His interest in Haven seemed sincere, and he wanted to know more about a board position. So far, he has brought in new sponsors and fulfilled his board member commitment. I hoped his youthful ambition would challenge seasoned members.

I pulled into the parking lot of the coffee shop. I didn't have any missed notifications on my cell. Mr. Brown sat by the window at a small table, dressed in Balmain, iPad in hand. He waved me over and stood for a hug as I approached the table. I tried to decline Damien's drink offer, but the assertive gentleman insisted. I chose an iced latte with white chocolate, caramel, and soy. Damien ordered an iced latte, too, but with caramel and almond milk. I tossed my cell phone in my handbag. Damien joined me back at the table with our drinks and straws.

"So, how's it been going? Not too brutal, I hope." His disarming charm made a good impression on screen that transferred well to his in-person demeanor. He tasted his drink, and his face perked up.

"I haven't had a call all afternoon. The statement we released satisfied the media, and the news coverage I've seen hasn't focused on Haven."

"Same, I've been browsing around, too." He ran his finger across the smudge-less screen, scrolling through news articles. "The center can't do much else but show support and answer any questions we can."

"Right." I took a long sip of my drink. I wished I could do more.

A slight shift in his posture. "I wanted to talk to you about the fundraiser." He leaned over to show me the clinic's website.

"Okay, what's this?" I waited.

"I know the board has concerns with timing, and rightfully so. I just wanted to see how you felt about maybe not throwing the idea away completely."

"They just want to postpone the discussion, but I'm open to your ideas. We need to focus on monetary commitments if we want this organization to survive."

"Well, I don't have anything flushed out yet, but this local clinic is interested in donating significantly." Damien clicked on the About Us section and scrolled to a headshot of a polished, friendly-looking physician.

"Oh, okay, go on."

"It's a verbal commitment, but I feel that the owner is serious. He talked about a family member who received help from Haven for a drug addiction."

"We could use another partnership with a clinic, and it's great the doctor has a personal connection." I picked up my cup. The barista made it extra sweet.

"He didn't give the name of the family member."

"No, of course not. Well, I'm glad the center was able to help. I wonder how long it's been."

"I'm not sure." He sipped his latte a third of the way down.

"No, it's fine. Thank you for reaching out to me. Would you be interested in training the board?"

"I don't know how everyone would receive that." We almost choked on our drinks as we drained our glasses.

Damien and I continued throwing ideas about the center's direction, mixed in with mindless chit-chat before we left the coffee shop. I texted Ian, the guy I had been seeing for several months, to see if we could have dinner tonight. I missed my sweet but rugged companion.

I had been in my apartment for over an hour, rummaging through my bags and work nook. I misplaced my flash drive. Before meeting with Ian, I planned to work on some clients' exit forms. I sent him a message.

Hey babe, so sorry, but we might have to postpone. I can't find my drive.

NP sweetie. Text me later. Look under your cookie stash.

I did.

I was walking around with the flash drive when one of our medical professionals stopped me to discuss a patient. Many times, I preached to staff about handling confidential information. I hopped out of my slippers and into some trainers, opting to stay in the joggers and pullover, and drove back to the center.

The tires crunched the gravel of the lot, and headlights flashed across the dark-tinted windows of the recovery center complex. I left the beeping sound of the doors locking behind in the cool night air as I took out my badge to access the administration door. My presence triggered the lights, brightening the dark office. A door closed in one of the back offices. It was after-hours, and none of the staff reported they'd be working late. I grabbed a tape dispenser on a nearby table. I crept down the hallway and forced the door open, vibrating the room as it slammed against the wall.

"Marsha, what are you doing here?" She was leaning over my desk, closing the drawer where she had put the money bag for me to verify the deposit amount before she went to the bank.

"I-I was putting it back." She stammered.

"Putting what back?" I questioned.

"The cash."

"You took the money?"

"I've been having financial difficulties. It was only to tie me over until I got paid."

"You should have talked to me about it instead of stealing. We could have worked something out." I wondered how long it had been going on. "What were you thinking?"

"I'm so sorry." She cried out.

The lights went out in the hallway, and the room grew cold. I didn't know what to say.

"It was the first time, I promise." She babbled like a child who hadn't yet mastered the formation of words.

"Do you realize what kind of position this puts me in? I always praise you to staff and the board."

"I know. I'll take all the heat for it. You didn't know anything about it."

"No, I didn't!"

She fiddled with her sleeves and attempted to iron out wrinkles by running her hands down the front of her dress. "I'll pack my things."

I didn't protest. "Just go." I felt like I was in the middle of a break-up.

"But, what about my things?"

"I don't have time for that right now."

She stepped out of the room and into the hall, pausing a moment to speak. I remained silent.

I took the money bag home until I could go to the bank. I didn't believe this was Marsha's first time taking from the center. She had been handling Haven's in-hand donations for the past few years. I shuddered at the thought. The rest of the night was useless. I didn't get any work done and barely slept; my mind traveled in multiple lanes, trying to decide my next move. I forgot about the flash drive and wanted to scream when I found it on the floor of my car under the driver's seat. If I had discovered it sooner, I would never have gone into the office and remained oblivious to my second in command's criminal activity.

Grant Guidry answered his cell after two rings. A drill ground through wood, and guys shouted back and forth. "Hey, what's going on?"

"Did I catch you at a bad time?" I hated bothering him when he was at a work site.

"No, it's fine." I heard shuffling, and then he asked me to hold on. One of the mission volunteers slowed their pace by my office door but kept moving when he saw I was on a call.

When Grant clicked back over, he barked orders to his employees. "They don't want that tile anymore in the kitchen." There was a brief pause. "It's in the back of the truck. Sorry about that."

I hated when people answered the phone and continued conversing with someone else. "Let's just talk another time."

"No, Chell, it's fine." Grant was a first cousin, sometimes more like a brother; our mothers were sisters. "I just need to make sure my guys use the right materials." The shuffling of his employees moved farther away. "So, how are you?"

"I'm good despite everything going on." An email popped up at the top of my inbox list. One of the accountants sent an updated report.

"Yes, of course. Any more news on what happened?"

"Nothing yet." I tapped my fingers on the desk, staring at the unread email. "Uhm." I hesitated, not sure how to word my question. "Have you heard from Marsha lately?"

"No. I can't remember the last time we talked." He thought it over. "I think she texted me yesterday, but I've been so busy."

"Oh, okay."

"Is everything good?"

"Not really." I opened the email.

"What happened?" I sensed a little excitement in his voice. "Nobody got hurt, huh?"

"No, it's nothing like that." The report showed a ten thousand dollar decrease in projected donations.

"Spit it out, girl," he commanded.

I turned my chair away from the computer, facing the back wall. "Marsha has been stealing money from Haven." A loud noise filled my ear. My cousin cursed before addressing me again. I lowered my cell's volume.

"You made me drop my phone in the back of the truck. Not, Marsha?!" They attended the same church, and according to Grant, she was an active and respected member.

"Yep. I caught her putting the money back in my office. I don't know how long it's been going on."

"Oh wow." Grant was silent for a moment. "I had no idea."

"Me, neither." An inspirational wooden sign hung above my back cabinet. Marsha had bought one for all the employees.

"She's a good person, you know." Grant sympathized.

"I know she is. That's why this is so difficult."

"Did you fire her?"

"Not yet."

"I understand."

"I don't know what I'll do without her, especially now."

"You got this. It'll work out." My cousin was among the first people I called when the tragedy hit the news. "Maybe she got spooked with the police coming around."

"You're probably right."

"Damn, I recommended her, too."

"It's not your fault."

"I still can't believe it."

I went silent. I considered bringing up Khristian Babineaux's confession.

"Have you talked to your dad lately?" My cousin diverted the conversation.

"No, not lately. Why?"

"Just asking."

I swung my chair back around and unlocked my computer screen, typing hard on the keys. "I didn't mean to talk this long."

"It's cool." One of the workers called out his name.

Grant went back to his remodeling project. I emailed the staff, stating Marsha would be out due to personal reasons.

CHAPTER 10

AUGUST 1995

Helena Richard walked about the kitchen, wiping any spots she missed on her first round. Her husband closed the door to his office and sat down at the dining table, flipping through an office furniture catalog. Charla sat in the living room listening to hip-hop. Chelsea entered the foyer, dragging the Skip It, which was still attached to her leg.

"Don't scratch my floors with that thing." Her mother warned. "Bring it up to your room and get washed up." Helena pointed up the stairs. "Charla!" She yelled but didn't get a response. She pulled the headphones off her older daughter's bobbing head. "Go get cleaned up. We're about to eat."

The family sat around the dining table, their plates loaded with chicken alfredo and fresh Caesar salad.

"Can we still go to the mall?" Charla begged her parents.

"Yeah." Chelsea chimed.

"That's up to your mother." Their father stopped on a page featuring an office chair.

"Maybe next weekend. I don't feel up to it."
Helena sighed.

"Ah, Mom, a couple of my friends are going to
see Mortal Kombat." Charla pleaded.

"Justin will be there." Chelsea kissed the air.
"Aww, cher," she teased.

"Quit it, Chell!" Charla reached for her younger
sister to end her ridiculous smooch fest.

"Arrête ça!" Helena chastised.

Charla shoved some salad in her mouth while
Chelsea chewed pasta, letting a noodle dangle on her chin.

"Erika is going to see Pocahontas, and I told her
we were going," Chelsea whined.

"You and your friend just want to go to the
cinema, because my friends and I are going. You always
go to the arcade like the other little kids."

"You play in it, too. You've only been thirteen for
a month, so." Chelsea stuck out her tongue, dropping a
piece of lettuce on her plate.

"Whatever." Charla rolled her eyes, pushing her
plate away. "You're still nine, so."

"I'll be ten next month, thank you." Chelsea put
her fork down.

"If y'all keep this up, we're not going anywhere."
Helena got up from the table, collecting her and Charles'
dishes. The sisters trailed their mother toward the
dishwasher, plates and glasses in hand.

"They can go." Their father surrendered, slapping
the catalog on the table and leaning back in his chair.

"Oh, well, I guess it's a yes." Their mother
responded.

"Let me get my wallet." Their father got up from
the table.

"I need to return an outfit anyway," Helena said before closing the dishwasher.

The girls ran to their rooms to get ready, forgetting all about their little tiff.

Helena pulled into the parking lot of the mall. She turned toward the backseat, handing her daughters the cash their father had allocated. Charla took her portion, calculating the movie ticket price and a pair of earrings. Chelsea slipped her money into her clear purse decorated with sunflowers, ready to hop out of the car. She asked if they could go to the waterfall at center court so she could toss a coin and make a wish. Their mother agreed, and they walked in that direction along the smooth, shiny cobblestone floor. Charla complained about needing to search for her friends but tossed a quarter in when her mother and sister weren't looking.

They walked towards the food court near the mall cinema. As they got closer, whiffs of cookie sweetness tempted their tastebuds. A chatty couple walked past them carrying trays loaded with Philly Cheesesteak subs and fries. Charla jumped up and ran over to a small group of girls. Helena smiled at an adult male towering over the young teens, the father of one of the friends.

Erika appeared like magic, dashing through the mall crowd toward them, her mother in tow. The bubbly child wore large-rimmed plaid glasses. She hugged Helena after releasing Chelsea.

The energetic companions shrieked and giggled while waiting for their movie tickets. Charla waved at her mom and sister; her group walked toward an opposite theatre. Helena explained to Erika's mother that she needed to return a dress and would return in a few minutes to join them.

"Of course, no problem. We're a bit early for our feature, and they always have so many previews." Mindy Simon had a high-pitched voice, and her swift words sprinted through the air. "We'll do a little window shopping while we wait." Helena had spoken to Mindy a few times at their daughters' school and when they came over for one of Chelsea's birthday parties.

Helena was relieved that no one was in the checkout line. She put the new dress on the counter and explained to the associate that it wasn't the right fit. She searched her purse for the receipt, shutting her eyes tight when she realized she left it on the bedroom dresser.

"I forgot the receipt." She apologized to the associate.

"I'm sorry, I will need a receipt if you want a refund unless you want to exchange it. Are the tags still on?"

"Yes." The department store crowd was growing, and she didn't have time to shop around. She could return to the house in under a half hour. Helena excused herself from the counter, took the dress, and said she would return with the receipt. She hurried through the mall and back out into the parking lot.

Charles Sr. was concealed in his office, shuffling through paperwork, when his pager beeped. He hung his head down, cursing the floor when he got the message. He reluctantly picked up the phone receiver, balancing it between his ear and shoulder. The high-pitched wails of the woman made him cringe. Her helpless tone was a far cry from her usual stern demeanor.

"It must be bad. You're not one to beg."

"My boss fired me," Yvette confessed.

"Why?"

"I don't know. I got haters, alright."

"There must be a reason. People don't just get fired."

"That manager been tryin' to get with me. I don't want his ass, so he started writin' me up. Okay?"

"Sounds like you didn't play your cards right." Charles joked.

"You think this is funny?" Yvette yelled. "I'm under a lot of stress raisin' our son. I make sure he gets to school and all these activities he joins. Some more money would help."

"I thought you didn't need my lil' check." Charles retorted.

"Look! I know what I said. You don't need to remind me."

"Ask one of those men you sleep around with for extra money."

"Why are you worried about who is in my bed?!"

"Trust me, I'm not." He dismissed her accusation. "What have you been doing for money? You better not have any drugs around him."

"Fuck you! You don't know what I do. You can't judge me." Her tone reached a screeching level.

"This money is for Chad."

"The amount I give is more than enough to care for his needs. You are not slick."

"You want him out on the street?! This is about him, I said!" Her wild screams forced him to pull the receiver away.

"What are you talking about?"

"I'm about to get evicted. We don't have anywhere else to go." Inaudible mumbling on the other end. "Did you hear what I said?" She blared.

"Watch your tone! I promise you won't get anything if you keep stepping out of line." Charles turned his chair around, squeezing his stress ball. "If you had done what I told you to do long ago, this wouldn't be a problem!" When Yvette told him she was pregnant, he didn't want to believe it was his child. He offered to pay for an abortion, but she refused. The paternity test confirmed this fling would be long-term.

"Oh, ohhhhh!" The woman's rage sped up. "Get rid of my baby-never!" She got up from the stained sofa she perched on. "Chad! Get over here and listen to how this cheatin' ass nigga feels about you!" She shoved the receiver at her son, who refused to take it. "That's your daddy!" Yvette's acrylic grip dug into Chad's arm, not releasing him until he took the phone.

"Hello." The eight-year-old spoke into the phone.

Charles didn't say anything at first. Chad's voice made him wish he could retract the careless words. He was torn between his disdain for the mother and his obligation to his son. "I'm sorry about this."

"You would say that about your son!" Yvette was back on the line. "Your own damn son!" She chanted her last words, inciting a response.

"I know he is my son!" Charles growled. He slammed the receiver down on the desk. Charles forgot his surroundings; the desk and all its contents had gone.

Helena stood in the doorway, the clear plastic cover protecting the dress draped over her arm. She shook the keys in her hand.

Charles jumped up. He felt dizzy as he waited for his thoughts to come around. He graced the desk with his fingers before gripping the edges. His wife moved back, away from the office, and out into the hallway. Helena found out about the affair when they were in Pensacola, but her husband hadn't confessed to having a son. Charles wanted to stop her and explain, but she was already down the stairs and out the door.

Helena entered the theatre; Pocahontas was just starting. Three silhouettes of her daughter, Erika, and Mindy sat in a row near the aisle. Helena walked over, back straight and head held high.

"Hey, mom!" Chelsea cried out, forgetting the quiet rule. Erika waved as she shoved popcorn into her mouth.

"Hey baby," Helena whispered, holding her finger to her mouth.

"Is everything okay?" Mindy asked as she made room for Helena to sit next to her.

"Yes, the line was ridiculous, and they had issues with the register."

"Oh, okay. You didn't miss much," Mindy assured.

Helena was thankful for the darkness. The show's animated images danced across the screen. She waited for the antidepressant she took on the way back to kick in.

CHAPTER 11

OCTOBER 2023

CHAD

Working for myself had its benefits. The flexibility of my schedule was worth the hustle and grind. I don't miss being attached to a desk all day. Confined spaces weren't my thing. I bounced around a lot as a child. We never stayed in one place for more than two years. The rent was paid one month, new furniture was staged, and name-brand clothes hung in the closet. The next, we might be out on our ass. My mom's sister Evelyn, who raised me to call her Aunt Lyn, complained about how much Yvette changed apartments. She said it wasn't good for me at that age. We never could stay with my aunt. She and her husband had their hands full with four kids. I liked to sit in a small section of my closet between my shoes and the wall. I wrote or drew using a flashlight as my guide. I often retreated to my creative space when Yvette had company. I didn't mind when they forgot about me. I grew to like being invisible.

I sat in the back of the neighborhood restaurant that I discovered had fire wings and loaded fries. I was working on a website for an international client who wanted an American appeal but needed a break from my apartment and something to satisfy my hunger. A small group walked in, and I hoped they wouldn't sit by me; there were plenty of open benches and tables. They settled for a worn bench near the front door. A waiter stepped from behind the counter and walked over to the customers. I needed a drink refill and another order of fries. The three miles I planned to run tomorrow would take care of that. I waved the worker over after he took the group's order. I checked my cell phone. I had a missed call from Yvette. I sent her a text.

> I'm in the middle of something. What you need?

Nuthin'-just checkin' on u. I ain't heard from u in days.

> It's a hectic time. I'll call you later.

K

One of the women in the group who sat at the end of the bench slipped her foot out of her shoe and rubbed the leg of the man across from her. He had his arm around the female next to him. The secret companions kept up with the pace of the conversation at the table while keeping their foreplay hidden.

Voyeurism is beneficial. You saw things people wanted to keep hidden. Social stalking is a given nowadays; amateurs do it, but nothing beats watching people in real time. Social media boasts those magazine moments. I preferred old-fashioned dirt, the truth behind the post. People have a mask for every occasion. COVID taught us that.

One morning, I was in a park, and a truck abruptly turned into the parking lot. A wobbling woman exited before the driver sped off. She stumbled a bit, trying to get her bearings, when something made her walk to the car beside her. She dug around in the vehicle for a bit. I moved in closer, careful not to alert her. When she popped her head out of the car's window, I backed off slowly and crept back to my car, which was on the other side of the lot. The unsteady woman moved toward one of the large old trees where a dead woman sat against a tree. The scared woman made a loud thump when she fell to the ground. She cried out before getting up. She walked quickly back to her car and started the engine, staring at the wheel for a few minutes before driving out of the lot. I followed her to an apartment building that reminded me of the outdated, in-need-of-repair complexes I lived in as a kid. She didn't earn much as a waitress at a wings and fries joint.

The woman from the park headed my way, ready to hand me the to-go order of fresh steak cut fries drizzled in barbecue sauce, spicy queso, bacon bits, and a side of ranch dip.

"Hi, handsome." Alexis Landry smiled, handing me the bag. "Here are your fries."

"Thank you, love."

Her long box braids sat atop her head in a tight bun. She reminded me of Yvette. Alexis took advantage of her full figure, exposing cleavage in a low V-neck top, snatched waist and tight jeans shaped her big ass.

"You're welcome, boo." She stayed leaned over the table and winked.

I left the restaurant with a food bag and Alexis' cell number saved on my phone. I called Yvette when I got in my car.

"You too busy to talk to yo momma."

"I'm working on a few projects."

"Well, that's good. Make that money."

"That's what you taught me." I maneuvered slowly from the restaurant parking lot, carefully avoiding the deep potholes.

"At least I taught you somethin'."

"Oh, yeah."

"Aside from that, you okay? Every time we talk, you in a different place." Yvette yelled to someone in the background.

"I'm good. You know I travel a lot. Never in one place for too long." I didn't like Yvette keeping tabs on me.

"I understand." A deep voice responded to her outburst. I suspected it was her latest dude. "Are you going to come and see me soon?" She said back on the phone.

"I don't know if it'll be soon, but I'll visit." I wanted to get on with this conversation to the part where she asked for money.

"Okay, I know how you get when you workin'." She seemed disappointed. "Everything is okay here," she volunteered. "It's just the a/c unit been actin' up."

And there it was. My mother lived in a rented house. Her part-time job at a convenience store covered food and utilities. I got tired of asking why she couldn't get a full-time job.

"The nigga in your house can't take care of that?" I honked at the car in front of me. The driver didn't move when the light turned green.

"You know Lester is waitin' on the settlement."

Bullshit. Yvette wasn't pulling them like she used to. The mother I knew would never be with a man who wasn't paying. Lester called out to Yvette, and she asked me to hold, putting the phone on mute.

A door slammed shut as Yvette unmuted the phone. Her slippers shuffled quickly across the floor. "I'm back."

"How much is it going to cost?" I didn't like footing the bill for a grown man to stay in my mother's home, yet I played the dutiful son.

"The first quote I got was way too high, but I can call 'round and compare."

"Okay."

"You sure you don't mind? I know it won't be cheap." Sometimes, Yvette had a way of getting you to do things without making a direct ask. The one time I remember when she did ask for something was when we were about to be evicted, and she was on the phone with my father. She kept me close while she and him went back and forth, throwing blows across the line. She put me on the phone at one point. My father had said something that made her angry. Later that day, I remember she paced back and forth in front of the apartment, smoking a cigarette, something she rarely did. She hated the smell, and it triggered my asthma.

"Just text when you get a price, and I'll see what I can do." I parked in a store lot.

"Okay, thank you, my baby."

I hadn't been her baby for a long time. "I have to go; another call is coming in. It's work." There was no call. I just didn't have time for fake affectionate shit.

"Okay, then. I'll text you soon."

"That works."

CHAPTER 12

CHARLA

Cindy sat across from me, leaning on my desk, craning her neck toward my computer screen. It was our routine meeting to go through reports. I clicked through the open tabs and highlighted some things that needed correction. Cindy will send me the updated report for final approval.

"So, how is your sister doing?" Cindy leaned back in the chair.

"She's good, all things considering." I closed the worksheet and pulled up my email to send her the updated version. I printed some account forms. "Working with the people at the center means a lot to her."

"I know." My accountant agreed. "It helps so many people." She walked over to the printer. "My younger brother struggled with substance abuse for years."

"I remember you told me that. Is he better now?"

"Yes, thank God." Cindy organized the printouts and slid them into a folder. "He's married with two kids. Sometimes, I think that if he hadn't got help, he wouldn't be here today, nor would my nephews."

"Thank God is right. I'm glad that he's doing well and has a family." An old college picture of Chelsea, me, and her childhood friend Erika sat atop a table at the back of my office. "Everyone that struggles with addiction doesn't get a happy ending."

"That's so true." She pondered the reality. "My brother is blessed." She leaned on the door frame.

Cindy and her husband had been trying to have a baby for years. She started IVF treatments again recently.

"Your blessing is coming," I assured.

Cindy nodded but remained silent, tapping the folder against her leg. Sometimes, we say things we think people want to hear. I had no control over whether my accountant would ever have a child, nor did she. I was surprised by the confidence in my inspirational words. I met her husband when he came to the office to pick her up when they were down to one car. Cindy's car needed a new engine. He seemed like a good man. A message from my boss popped up on my screen. He wanted to make changes to a meeting agenda.

"What are you having for lunch?" Cindy stepped out into the hall.

"My sister asked me to join her for some Thai food."

"Oh, that sounds good."

I couldn't decide on whether to ask Cindy to join us, but she chose for me. "I know the two of you have things to discuss. I'll probably walk down to the café on Coolidge and get a shrimp wrap and fries."

"Now, that sounds delicious. I love their salsa cream."

"Me, too!" Cindy smiled before walking back to her desk.

Chelsea and I sat in the Thai restaurant on Johnston Street. It was her spot until she got me hooked. The pad se ew was delicious. Skipping sweets is easy for me, but the fried banana rolls with coconut ice cream are a must-order. I got it along with the sweet, thick, savory noodles and beef. My sister opted for the medium spicy red curry with chicken.

"So, what's been going on?" I questioned after the server brought our meals.

"A lot." Chelsea took a sip of her iced tea and handed me her phone.

"I thought things with the news story slowed down. No one is harassing you, right?"

"No, nothing like that." She pointed to the opened text on the screen. "One of our therapists just turned in his resignation via text."

"Oh wow." I skimmed through the message."

"He's going into private practice with a partner."

"Well, he's not professional." I put her cell on the table. I stabbed the batch of sweet, saucy noodles and beef.

"We're already short-staffed." Chelsea griped, murdering a spoonful of chicken curry and rice.

"That's nothing new. Most of your therapists don't stay longer than a year or two." They used Haven for experience building and community support boasting.

Chelsea picked up her cell and scrolled through her photo gallery. She held it up, showing me a picture of the staff standing in front of the center.

"Okay." I'd already seen it on Haven's social media page.

She spread her fingers to zoom in. It was a close-up of a counselor, Khristian Babineaux. "He just told me that he and Brienne had history."

"What? What kind of history?"

"They went to the same college and dated for a bit."

"And he never said anything until now?" I sipped on my iced water with extra lemon.

"Nope. He explained that he reached out when he realized she was a client, but she wanted to keep their past private."

"I wonder why." My mind ran through a list of reasons as I swirled more noodles around my fork.

"He also said something about how she used things against people."

"Khristian is a bit strange. You never know. Maybe Brienne had something on him."

"He admitted as much."

"Do you think he's connected to her death?" I never liked the weird counselor; his recent confession didn't help my suspicions.

"I don't know what to think. He said their involvement was ages ago, and he doesn't know what happened to her. Plus, the police haven't said anything to me about him or made an arrest." Chelsea scooped up chicken and rice.

"I see." Khristian remained on my suspect list.

"I also got an email from a long-time partner that said they wouldn't be able to support this year."

"Who?"

"One of the health systems."

"Maybe it's financial reasons, Chell. Businesses are still struggling after the pandemic."

"They just donated $50K to a homeless shelter."

"Listen, businesses change their philanthropic contributions all the time. I'm sure it's not personal."

"At this point, I don't know." Chelsea snatched her glass of tea.

One of the servers checked to see if we needed anything. I reached for my cell in my bag. I showed my sister a picture of her niece. Dede baked sugar cookies and was covered in flour, with sprinkles scattered in her hair.

"How did the cookies taste?" Chelsea laughed.

"Surprisingly good. She has skills."

"Have you talked to dad lately?" My sister interjected.

I wondered what made her ask the question. She stayed in touch with our father more often than I did.

"Not lately, why?"

"Just asking." She waved off any of my preconceived notions. "Grant asked about him."

"Oh, you talked to Grant; how's he doing with his wild self?"

"Still crazy as ever."

"How's Marsha been doing?" I snuck in. "You haven't talked about your assistant in a while." She gulped her tea and coughed when it went down the wrong way. "You okay?"

"Yeah," she choked, clearing her throat before taking another sip. "Marsha has been out lately."

"I hope it's not an emergency."

"I caught her in the office." My sister spoke in a hushed whisper.

"Caught her doing what?" I scooped up some coconut ice cream and a bit of banana roll.

Chelsea wiped away some curry sauce from her mouth before responding. "She's been taking money from the center. I saw her putting it back."

"What?!" The shock was evident in my tone. Two ladies seated at a nearby table stopped in mid-conversation.

"Yeah. She told me some story about having financial trouble."

"I can't believe she's been stealing, but this explains why she never sent me the latest report." Chelsea sighed in agreement. I knew she treasured her working relationship with Marsha. "Did you fire her? Are you going to file a report?"

"Not yet. I put her on immediate leave."

"With pay?"

Chelsea didn't offer a yes or no. "She claims she put it all back."

"It doesn't matter. Chell-" I started, but she cut me off.

"I didn't say I believe her." She snapped at me. "That's what I've been dealing with, in addition to this other stuff. The last thing I need is for you to walk me through firing one of my employees." She pinned down a strip of chicken with her fork.

"Trust me. I get it." I tried to calm her down. "Letting someone go is not easy. I've had to do it before."

"Okay, then just back off a little." She ate the rest of her food quietly, not wanting to continue the conversation.

CHAPTER 13

CHELSEA

It felt strange not having Marsha in the office. Staff questioned her absence. I kept them busy, delegating additional duties, and helped pick up some slack. I wasn't a fan of answering the phone, organizing documents, completing forms, or reviewing applications. The list went on. Despite what Marsha did, I appreciated her work but couldn't continue with the extra workload.

I picked up my cell. I had a notification from Iman Anderson, one of my friends from college. She was excited about a guy she met named Sean. Every man Iman met was the one.

How long has this been going on?

2 mos now. We've been on a few dates.

Ohhh, nice. Details later, please.

Of course. He surprised me with flowers today-box checked!

> *That's so sweet. I'm happy for you.*

A calendar alert popped up. It was my 5:00 PM appointment with an applicant for a therapist position. I grabbed my makeup bag and a comb and headed to the bathroom to freshen up. I pulled some paper towels from the dispenser to dry off my hands when my watch vibrated. It was Ian. I promised him we could meet after work. He was going to get tired of me canceling dates. I sent Ian a message asking if we could postpone our meet-up time. I finished reapplying my makeup and headed out of the bathroom. Ian hadn't responded.

The dapper Franklin Johnson sat with his legs crossed, hands clasped on his lap. He was in his thirties, with boyish charm, confident, not arrogant. I imagined Mr. Johnson could carry a meeting in a board room with senior white collars just as easily as he could work a classroom filled with high school teenagers.

"What made you apply to Haven?" I crossed my arms on the desk; his CV and reference letters were in front of me.

"I want to help give people the tools to get back on their feet and live again."

Good answer, but not unlike the responses of other applicants. "Do you have a personal connection with substance abuse?"

"My mother battled with a drug addiction for years. It made it hard for her to raise me." He uncrossed his legs and pushed the glossy black twists out of his face. "I lived with my grandmother for a while."

"Thanks for sharing that you have firsthand experience with substance abuse. I know how tough it can be to see a loved one struggle."

"It is. That's why I love what you do here. My mom was a new person after she got treatment."

"I'm so glad to hear that." I picked up one of his reference letters. "Tell me about your volunteer counseling experience at this trauma center." I listened to Franklin talk about the troubled youth he helped. Ian still hadn't replied to my text.

"I want people dealing with addiction to feel worthy and deserving of a second chance. That's the message I tried to instill in the kids at the center."

"I love your passion." I smiled.

"Thank you." He relaxed his posture.

The interview went on a little longer than I expected. I told Franklin that I would be in touch, and I meant it. I got in my car and called Ian.

"Hey." His voice was dry.

"Hey, yourself. I texted you back. I had an interview."

"Well, I had a busy day, too." He countered.

"You okay?"

"I'm good."

"It doesn't sound like it."

"Look, I had a rough day."

"Do you still want me to come over?"

"Yeah, that's fine."

The inside of Ian's home was vintage meets contemporary modern. He gave me a warm hug and kiss.

I handed him the bottle of wine I picked up on the way. I ruffled his thick, black, curly hair, making him smile.

"I interviewed a guy about a therapist position." I took off my shoes and hopped on the couch. "Remember I told you how the last one quit."

"Yeah." Ian put the bottle of wine in the kitchen and scrolled through his phone.

"I hate having to schedule all these interviews. Plus, I need a new assistant!" I threw myself back on the couch. The ceiling fan blades circled slowly. Ian grunted in agreement, seated on a kitchen barstool, still searching his phone. "Are you even listening to me?"

"Yes, I am." He paused. "Like I always do."

"What's that supposed to mean?" I leaned over the sofa.

"Nothing." He walked over to kiss me on the forehead, but I pulled away.

"No, say what's on your mind."

"It's that listing I told you about." Ian got his real estate license a few years ago to bring in extra income, but it proved more lucrative than a basic side hustle.

"These sellers could have sold this property long ago if they weren't so stubborn." He sat down next to me.

"What's going on?"

"They don't want to budge from the initial listing price."

"How much do they want?"

"Three million. They just refused a cash offer for 2.5."

"I know that's frustrating."

"Yes, it is. It's been a while since I had a closing. My broker is on my back."

"I didn't realize that." I sympathized.

Ian locked the screen and set his phone on the end table before turning back to me." "You know I'm here for you. I just have some stuff going on, too."

"I'm sorry. I got caught up in all this mess."

"I understand. It's fine." He pulled me over to sit on top of him for a sweet embrace. His skilled lips made it easy to reciprocate. I unbuckled his pants, hardening his erection. Ian unclamped my bra and slid it up my arms. He leaned me backward and softly kissed my breasts and stomach.

"Want to take this to the shower?" I whispered.

"Definitely." He took me by the hand and led me to the bathroom. Ian picked me up, threw me against the shower wall, removed our soaked clothes, and tossed them on the floor.

CHAPTER 14

AUGUST 1995

CHAD

It was a few days after the fight with my dad. Yvette grabbed the cordless phone off the wall base and punched numbers with her thumb. She bit her nails as she waited for the person to pick up, repeating, "Come on, pick up." Moments later, my mother ranted into the phone to her sister about what happened, with more cursing and exaggerated body movements than before.

"I'll drive over there!" She shouted, then listened briefly, pacing in the kitchen and shoving a dirty pot in the sink. "I guess I am crazy, then!"

Her attention off me, I went to my room, closed the door, grabbed my sketch pad, and sat in the closet. I could still hear some of the conversation through the wall. I flipped my pad open to a clean sheet and closed my eyes to picture the burger joint my father took me to, with the outdoor seating covered by umbrellas. I tried my best to recreate it, starting with one large square and then drawing another on the top part of the way down, connecting the points with a line and the same with the bottom, as we learned in art class. I made a long rectangle across the top of the 3-D-looking box for the roof and then filled it with smaller squares to make what my father said were shingles. I heard a loud bang against the living room wall and another as an object hit the floor. I closed my pad and hung my head down, hoping she didn't break the phone.

Yvette came busting in and straight for the closet, yelling at me to stop acting weird and to get out of it. I stood in the middle of the room, holding my drawings close to my chest. My mother reached into the closet, pulled down a gym bag she had bought me last Christmas, and tossed it on my bed. She yanked open my dresser drawers and took out some shirts, shorts, and a few pairs of underwear.

"Are we going somewhere?" I asked.

"Yes, we are." She replied coldly.

"Where are we going?" I stuttered.

"You'll see when we get there." She stuffed the clothes in the bag. "Go get your toothbrush, toothpaste, deodorant, and one bar of soap from the bathroom." I didn't move fast enough. "Now!" I hurried out of the room to get the things she asked for.

In the early evening, we left Florida and drove for hours in my Aunt Lynn's car. She let my mother borrow it because her Camry needed new brakes. I had never been out of Florida before. My mother was born in Louisiana, but her family moved to Pensacola when she was a kid. I had a notebook in my lap and a bag of markers that I kept in a dark purple Crown Royal pouch that I got from Uncle Barry, one of my mom's older brothers. I wrote down the highway signs we passed: Mobile, Biloxi/Gulfport, Slidell,

New Orleans, and Baton Rouge. We stopped at a taco place on the way. Yvette reminded me that we weren't stopping again when I asked for a refill of my Pepsi.

I was asleep when she parked at the motel. I woke up to the slamming of the car door. "Get up, Chad!" She commanded, opening the backdoor. The warm night air tickled my skin. The a/c worked in this car, and Yvette kept it on the whole way. The person at the counter offered a cracked smile as she saw the wrinkled cash my mom dug out of her purse. "Okay, good." I heard Yvette say aloud as she placed the last bill on the counter. It was enough to cover the room. She took our key before we headed back out to the parking lot. Our room was at the back of the motel. We passed the pool, but she didn't pack my swimming trunks. The room had one large bed, and it looked clean. I put my gym bag on a chair while my mother threw hers on the bed. It was late. Yvette checked the bathroom and wiped the sink, toilet, and tub before we used them. After we washed and ate sandwiches and chips, she ordered me to go to bed, turning off the television before she settled under the covers.

I stared at the box of hot glazed donuts that Yvette had bought. The box had an image of a smiling donut wearing a crown. I just finished my first one. She saw me staring and passed the open box to me in the backseat without a fuss. She checked herself in the rearview mirror, wiping sugar from her mouth, reapplying red lipstick, and adjusting her thick gold chain. Her braids were loose, hanging down her back, and she wore a bright yellow crop top with most of the buttons open to show off her breasts and short jean shorts that I watched her cut even more. I looked down at my worn Lakers jersey and stained purple shorts. I wish she had packed better clothes. My mother drove for a while before admitting where we were going.

"We're going to see your father." My body tightened. I remembered how upset she was on the phone with him and the threats she made when talking to her sister. I started to kick my feet back and forth, hitting the back of the front driver's seat. "Kick the seat again and see." She pinched her lips together, threatening a whipping. She turned the car into a neighborhood with houses the size of our apartment building and cruised down one of the streets, checking the mailbox numbers. We stopped in front of a two-story white house with flower bushes lining the front. I recognized the SUV in the driveway and another expensive-looking car parked in front of it under the carport. I liked where my father lived. My mother got out quickly, opened the backdoor, and urged me to do the same. I pulled away from her, and she scolded me, reaching into the backseat. I shuddered at the thought of her American tips digging into my arms. I flung off the seatbelt and hopped out of the seat. I stood behind my mother as she knocked on the large wooden door with a glass window. A tall figure appeared. It was my father. He looked terrified as he scanned the front yard.

"Yeah, surprise!" Yvette started. I walked over to one of the bushes to touch the flowers.

"What the hell do you think you're doing?" My father stepped out in a red and black tracksuit, partially closing the door behind him.

"Think you can hang up on me like I can't find where you stay."

"You're crazy. I'll have you arrested."

"Okay, arrest me." She snatched me from the bush and positioned me between her and my father. "Arrest me in front of your son!" Her voice escalated, setting the scene.

My father locked eyes with me but quickly turned back to Yvette. "Look," he held his hand out as he chose his words, "we can talk about this somewhere else, but not here."

"You don't want your family to meet your son?"

"I'm not going to repeat it- "A tall woman appeared, opening the door and cutting my dad's sentence short. She looked like one of my schoolteachers, taller than my mother, not as curvy. She starched her clothes, and her bumped hair sat above her shoulders. I spotted two girls, one much shorter than the other, standing on the stairs.

"Well, here we go." My mother waved her arms in the air. I tried to get behind her, but she blocked my attempt, keeping me front and center.

The woman beside my father said something to him through gritted teeth. He moved away from her and charged Yvette, throwing her off guard. His larger frame forced her back towards my aunt's car. She cursed as she resisted him, getting attention from someone walking their dog. I followed them, keeping my head down. My father managed to get her in the car, keeping his body pressed against the front door so she couldn't open it. Yvette finally stopped screaming and sat resting her hands on the steering wheel. She started the car. Once my dad backed off the door, my mother motioned me over and shoved a piece of paper from the hotel in my hand before speeding off down the road. My father cursed under his breath and then apologized. He stayed facing the street, away from his house, putting his face in one hand, the other on his hip. After a few moments, he kneeled beside me, held my hand, and told me who the woman and girls were before he took me inside.

His daughters stared as I tripped on the rug in the foyer. "Hey," I said to the spotless wood floor, not knowing what else to do. The younger one, who looked about the same age as me, wore large pigtails, bright green overalls, and a white t-shirt, moved to approach me, but her mother whipped out a hand to stop her. The older flipped her hair behind her shoulders and glared at me through straight-edged bangs, standing tall in a plaid short dress and choker around her neck. She fiddled with a CD Walkman and took off her headphones. My father and his wife were arguing, moving their fight into the kitchen. It was much bigger than the one at the apartment, and it had a counter in the middle.

"What was I supposed to do? Leave him outside?" He shoved something across the counter.

"I don't care what you do, but you better get that little bastard out of my house!" His wife stormed out of the kitchen, ordering her daughters to go back upstairs. She entered the living room and didn't take her eyes off me, rearranging the statutes on the coffee table after I touched them.

No one ever called me a bastard before. The woman acted like one of those white master's wives in the slave movies Yvette rented saying I needed to know my history. His wife didn't want me in the house. I waited for her to order me back out into the fields.

Later that day, my father and I went to a store. I banged my head against the seat, wanting to disappear, as we drove to another hotel, a nicer one than where Yvette and I slept. "This isn't your fault." My father's voice was soft, like he cared, the opposite of how he spoke to my mother.

The next day, we were back in the SUV, and memories of when my dad took me to the burger place danced around in my head. We spent the day together, driving around Lafayette. He pulled up to a Chinese restaurant. We went inside this time. He didn't talk about how much food I put on my plate or how fast I ate.

"Can I stay with you?" I asked. He took a long time to respond. I moved the shrimp fried rice around on my plate with my fork.

My father looked across the table. "I wish things were different and you could stay with me, but-" He shook his head, not saying the word no.

It was late when he brought me back to Yvette's hotel. I had fallen asleep in the backseat but woke up to raised voices in the parking lot.

"Where have you been?!" My father barked. "I called your room twice."

"None of your business! I'm not your stiff wife." Yvette stood, crossing her arms.

"Don't talk about my wife!" he shouted, stepping toward her. "You smell like the club," he sniffed.

"Oh, please! That's how I met you."

"Please stop fighting all the time!" I exited the SUV, slammed the door, and headed for the room.

"Son!" My father called out, but I kept on walking.

"Chadwick!" My mother yelled, heels pricking the cement as she hurried after me.

The following day, Yvette and I drove back to the two-bedroom apartment with scratched walls, noisy pipes, and stinky air. Before we left the hotel parking lot, she took out the check my father gave her and held it up to the windshield, popping it open with a pleased expression.

"Way more than he usually gives." She grinned. "I know you're mad about what I did, but you don't understand." Her voice was shaky. "We needed this money."

"I know, it's whatever."

"I don't care what he says. He doesn't love you. You saw who he loves."

I turned to look out the window and closed my eyes.

"I'll get you some new clothes for school, and if you behave, those Nike sneakers you like." She reached back to touch my leg, but I moved it away.

CHAPTER 15

Charla and Chelsea sat in the back bedroom of their aunt's house. They stacked their luggage at the end of the bed. The walls were blue and littered with sports posters. A Sega Saturn console sat on a bottom shelf under the television. A metal chair was pushed into a cluttered desk with a black-based lava lamp and electric blue floating globs. Comic books and X-Men action figures staggered about. It was their cousin Grant's room. He and his dad were in Texas, visiting family. It was the first night the girls slept over. Chelsea sat on the floor, fixated on the television as the intro of The Secret World of Alex Mack came on. Charla lay on her stomach on the bed, kicking her legs up and down. She noticed the show coming on and closed the TEEN magazine.

Selene Guidry was cooking in the kitchen. She wore an oversized peach-colored top, cropped pants, and house slippers. The phone rang. It was Helena, her younger sister, and her third call of the day. "They're fine, cher, the same as before."

"Okay, okay." Their mother sighed into the phone. "I just wanted to make sure Charla packed her retainer; she hates wearing it."

Selene bowed and let out a low groan before speaking. "They're in the back watching TV. Let me go check." She put the receiver down. She was still talking loud enough for her sister to hear. "You better not cause me to let my sausage and tomato gravy burn."

Charla noticed her aunt enter the room. Chelsea focused on the screen.

"Hey, your mom is on the phone," Selene questioned Charla. "Did you pack your retainer?"

"Yes, Aunt Sellie," Charla threw her hands up. "She asked me that before we left the house."

"Yeah, I figured. You know she's nervous."

"Very."

"What did that lil' girl turn herself into, a liquid puddle or something?" Aunt Sellie aimed her question at the television, getting Chelsea's attention.

"That's Alex Mack. She can morph into goo, and she glows!" Her niece turned away from the television.

"Mais jamais." She made the sign of the cross, her superstition running wild. "Y'all children watch some strange things."

"It's cool. Sit down and watch." Chelsea begged.

"I have to get back to your mom and finish the food, but I'll return."

"Okay." Chelsea turned her attention back to the show.

"She has her retainer." Selene relayed back to her sister, picking up the receiver.

"Good." Helena paused for a bit. "I appreciate you watching the girls for a few days. I know school is about to start soon. I just didn't want them here while we try to sort this out."

"It's fine. I missed my nieces anyway, and they're not bad kids. I deal with enough of those in the classroom." They both laughed. "I took them to my mall yesterday."

"On the north side?" Helena laughed.

"Yes, there was a department store sale, and the girls wanted to check out the other shops."

"Did y'all buy anything?"

"Yeah, a few things." Selene glanced at the shopping bags that were still on the sofa. "You and Charles spoil these kids. They asked to go to the movies. I told them I'm not paying high for a ticket when we can go to the cinema on this end for a dollar."

"I'm sure they fussed about that."

"They went and had a good time." Selene boasted.

"I'll give you some money."

"No, don't worry about it. I know it's tough for you, but you do what you must. I told you Charlie was no good." Selene stepped onto her soapbox.

"I remember what you said but marrying him was what I wanted then."

"That's how it is. These men trap you with the song and dance before the ring, but real colors start to show once you say, I do."

"Yeah, I never thought he would do this, and he kept it from me for so long." Helena held back tears.

"Because he's a liar, like most of them." Selene snapped. "He risked losing his family for a night with a…" She peeked around the corner to see if her nieces were still in the back room. "A hoe."

"That's exactly what she is." Helena sniffled, tears drying up. "You should have seen how she was dressed, cutting up on the front lawn, and he slept with that."

"They don't care, cher." Selene stirred her sausage and red sauce before lowering the fire. She turned off the rice pot and checked on the cream-style corn.

"I regret what I said in front of the boy. He didn't deserve that."

"What did you say?"

"I said I wanted him out of the house." Her tone lowered. "Called him a bastard."

"Oh." Selene contemplated. "Technically speaking, he is."

"Sellie!" Helena chastised.

"Sadly, he heard that, but don't beat yourself up about it. You were angry and had every right to feel that way."

"I just couldn't stand to look at him."

"Understandably so. This whole mess is Charlie's fault."

"I think I've bothered you enough." Helena yawned.

"It's not a bother. Call anytime you need. I'm here."

"Okay, thank you again. Love you."

"Love you, too."

The ending credits rolled on the screen before a commercial appeared; the high-pitched voice annoyed their ears. Chelsea lowered the volume and looked around the room for something to play with. She went to the desk to check out the action figures and started rummaging through the drawers, looking for anything interesting. In the bottom drawer was a new pack of pens, a box of pencils, and a sharpener. She kept hunting, looking under the bed. There was a black shoe box. She pulled it out to see a stack of college rule notebooks. At the bottom, she saw the August 1995 Playboy cover, a red-haired woman in a sexy red and white polka dot outfit holding a vintage microphone. Chelsea covered her mouth, chuckling, and turned to show her sister. Charla took the magazine from her sister.

"Grant will have to pay us big time for this." Charla grinned as she flipped through the pages. She settled on a bookmarked page of a naked woman, and she imagined what Grant would be doing while he looked at it, and she threw it down on the bed, causing Chelsea to jump back. "Eeew!" She cried out.

"What?!" Chelsea questioned.

"You don't want to know." She went back to her TEEN magazine.

"You never tell me anything." Chelsea flipped through the television channels, searching for something else to watch.

"I'm not talking about it with you," Charla replied.

"I'm not stupid, you know." Chelsea stopped on the city's open channel; confederate flags and disguised men in hooded robes at a table caught her attention. It was The Klan of Akadiana, and a caller was shouting about white rights, earning cheers from the audience. "I hate this show. Why is it even on TV?"

"Because they're racist, and other racists support it." Charla looked up from her magazine. "Turn it off before Aunt Sellie sees. She'll get mad, and we'll hear about it for the rest of the night."

"Not all whites are racists." Chelsea thought about her friend Erika.

"No, not all. You have to learn people, Chell. Not everyone is your friend." Charla reached for the remote and changed the channel.

CHAPTER 16

OCTOBER 2023

CHARLA

I sat on the side of Dede's bed, taking her temperature. She had a slight fever that finally started to go down. I left work early to pick her up from school after getting the call she had thrown up. Dede opened YouTube on her iPad and selected an episode of Gracie's Corner.

"You can watch one episode, and then you need to sleep." She nodded in agreement, smiling as the show started. When her father called, I exited the room to get her a drink.

"Hey, Charla, how's it going?"

"It's not a good time. Dede caught a bug or something."

"Oh, why didn't you tell me?" Justin questioned.

"I had to pick her up early from school and contact the pediatrician. She just got settled in bed."

"Oh, okay, sorry. How is she doing?"

"Better, but she needs to get some rest."

"Okay, good."

Preston Smith's name popped up on my screen. "Hey Justin, I need to take this. I'll update you later."

"Uhm, okay, that's fine."

Preston was from Chicago. He was ambitious, full of fresh ideas, and spontaneity. It was a welcomed change from the men I had been coming across. I wondered what brought him to the boot. He was a sales manager for a software company. The company wanted to grow its clientele in the southern region.

"Good evening, gorgeous," he greeted. "How's little Nugget doing?"

"Good evening, charmer," I said sarcastically. I had shared my nickname for Delilah.

"Dede isn't feeling well. I think she caught a bug."

"Oh, no. Is it bad?"

"She's looking better than when I first picked her up at school."

"Maybe spending time with her mommy made her feel better. I know it makes me feel better."

"Someone is laying it on thick." I teased. "I like it, though."

"I know you do." He cooed. "I was calling to find out if I could see you tonight, but you're busy with mom duties, so I can't be too heartbroken."

"Nope," I teased, "but it won't be long before we see each other." Preston was a good dater. He was creative and thoughtful, not one for the default dinner and a movie. On our last date night, he set up a picnic with a decked-out charcuterie spread by the river; white lights bordered our blanket. Coltrane played from a portable speaker. At the night's end, he walked me to my car and

106

kissed my forehead, asking me to text when I got home. I hoped for a different ending the next time we saw each other.

I peeked in on Dede; she had fallen asleep, leaving Gracie and the squad to dance alone. I turned off the iPad and put it down on the nightstand. I thought about what my sister asked me at the restaurant. I hadn't spoken to my father in almost two months. The long periods without communication didn't faze me. He could do more to keep in touch; it can't always be on the children. I wondered if he kept in touch with his son. He never talked about him. I still remember that summer when that ghetto woman came to the house, swinging her hips and braids up and down the driveway, and the look on my mother's face. I had never seen my father look so terrified. I picked up my cell and dialed his number. He was in the middle of watching a football game.

"Do you want to call me back?"

"No, sweetie. My team is losing anyway, so it's fine." I heard his new lady friend in the background asking who was on the phone. "Yeah, that was Gayle. You know she asked me to dress alike to go to some party."

"Seriously?" I laughed. My father would never do that.

"So, how's my beautiful grandbaby doing?" His voice still boomed, but age had lowered the bass and tempo.

"Dede is on bed rest now. She was running a fever and threw up, but she's starting to feel better."

"Oh, no. Not my little energetic princess."

"She conned me into letting her watch Gracie's Corner, but I told her it would have to be from her bed.

107

She dances all over the living room when I put that show on."

"Yes," he giggled. "She showed it to me on her little pad."

Gayle returned, saying something about jambalaya and asking what drink he preferred. My father never turned down a plate.

"How is your sister? I usually hear from her more often."

"She has a lot going on with the center and the news."

"Yeah, yeah." His wheels started to turn. "I saw that on the news about that young girl. Awful, man."

"It is."

"Chell handling everything okay?"

"As best she can."

"The table is set." His girlfriend called out.

She was a persistent one. We said our goodbyes and ended the call.

Immediately after hanging up with my father, I called my mother. She was at home, but I didn't hear the usual low tone of her nighttime television shows or the humming of the air purifier she kept near the bed.

"How has your business course been going, professor?" I asked. She was an instructor at UL.

"It's going well." She sounded chipper as she boasted about her role. My mother stopped working full-time during the COVID shutdown and took part-time remote jobs.

"That's cool, mom. I'm happy for you."

"Thanks, sweetie. I am, too. Being back in person full-time still feels weird, but it's good for me."

"Are you sure you can handle those college students?" I teased.

"Can they handle me?" She joked.

Helena ran a tight ship, and once you got on board, you followed her navigation; alternate routes would get you thrown overboard. I heard a chuckle I didn't recognize and a muffled sound like the cell speaker was covered. My mother always struggled with the mute button.

"Who is that?" I questioned.

"No one, dear." Her voice was more precise, and nothing obstructed her words. "I'm messing with the ROKU channels, looking for a movie."

"Oh, okay." I didn't pry. I wondered if Helena had a friend.

CHAPTER 17

NOVEMBER 2023

CHAD

I walked around the woman's messy bedroom. The sheet partially covered her body revealing her cropped t-shirt and panties. I waited until she stopped stirring and closed her eyes before I searched her apartment. Alexis Landry was several years younger than me and noticeably more immature. Entertaining someone when you have nothing in common is draining. We had been texting back and forth for a couple of weeks now. In that short time, I learned that her job at the restaurant was her primary source of income, but she aspired to be an influencer. I quickly searched the knock-off handbags that lined the top shelf of her closet.

Alexis confessed that she saw the dead woman in the park. "He dropped me off in the parking lot that morning," she reached for a joint, trying to calm her nerves. "I don't know. I heard a phone go off and saw the car with the windows down." She puffed. "I heard something and walked over to the tree." She hugged her knees close to her chest as she described how scary it was to find the body. I jumped when she started to tear up; her level of emotion made me uncomfortable. I patiently waited until she pulled herself together, placing my arm around her shoulders as she sobbed, resting her head on my chest. I handed her another drink and watched as she guzzled it down, wiping her wet lips and smiling at me.

"I hate myself for not calling the cops!" She wailed.

"It's okay, you were scared." I kissed her neck and slid my hand under her shirt. "That doesn't make you a bad person." I peeked at my watch. It was getting late, and I needed to finish a website for one of my top clients.

"I kept her cell phone," she sniffled.

"You did? I questioned. "Where did you put it?"

Alexis got up, wobbling across the room to look for it, forgetting where she put it. Her search ended when I stood up to catch her from falling over. I sat her on the bed and let her fall back, positioning her head on the pillow and sliding her legs one atop the other.

I opened dresser drawers filled with bras, panties, and sleepwear. I looked in a stand beside the bed that housed a cell phone with a cracked screen, but it wasn't the one I wanted. I slid a sparkly phone case and charger aside. I picked up a couple of clear baggies of Xanax. I searched the laundry she had in a basket. I gave up on the bedroom and surveyed the living room and kitchen. I wasn't leaving without Brienne's phone.

It wasn't a coincidence when we ran into each other. I had been watching Brienne for a long time. It had been a few weeks since she moved out of Haven and got an apartment. I waited outside her loft and watched

111

her hop in the car, dressed for early morning gym workouts.

"I work for a marketing agency and have a second job as a waitress at night." The breathless Brienne shared as she jogged on a treadmill next to me. "What do you do?" She asked.

"I do a lot as a freelancer," I started, "but mostly cyber security."

"Oh wow." She hit the stop button on the machine, reaching for her water bottle. "I heard you can make a lot of money doing that."

"It pays well." I hopped off the treadmill and wiped my face down with a towel.

"Have you found a church here yet?" She stood next to me, drinking from the bottle.

"No, not really."

"Would you like to try mine out?" She seized the moment.

"Sure." I agreed. It's not like I hadn't been to church before. When Yvette dated a churchman, we went to a few services, and she got what the howling congregation called saved. I never saw my mother act like that before. When I noticed he stopped coming over, and his phone calls ceased, I asked her about it. All she said was that she couldn't compete with Jesus. Brienne and I kept the relationship light initially. That allowed for a natural escalation.

Alexis stirred, dribbling inaudible words in her sleep. I moved faster. I hadn't searched the coat closet. I opened the door and looked around. There was a small box on the top rack. I put on my jacket and slid the phone into my pocket. I felt around for my car fob and then remembered it fell on the floor in the living room when Alexis jumped me seconds after we got inside her place. I kneeled and felt around under the couch until I seized it. I slipped on my cap and stepped out into the night, pushing the inside door handle lock before exiting.

CHAPTER 18

NOVEMBER 2023

Alexis got up the following day, and her spinning head fell back onto the pillow, disjointed thoughts jumbled around. She tried to piece together the broken fragments. She met him at a bar, the guy who always ordered the wings and loaded fries. They talked over drinks, and he asked to go to her place. Alexis threw the cover over the empty spot next to her, scrolling through their message thread in her cell phone that went back only a couple of weeks. "Shit!" She shouted, noticing the time. She was late for work the second time this week.

Alexis opened a message and started to text her boss, making up a reason for being late again. She deleted it before hitting send, afraid of her boss's response. She went back to the message thread with the wing and fry guy.

> Guess u had to run out. I know
> u busy. I'm kool wit hangin'
> out again."

After waiting a few minutes and not receiving a response, she returned the cell phone to the table and went to the bathroom to shower.

The small old-school restaurant wasn't too busy when she arrived. She didn't see her boss when she walked in. The cook glanced up from the grill, offered a half smile, and went back to flipping. One of the other servers was in, hanging out in the back on his phone, waiting for an order to bring to the one table with customers. He looked up, breaking away from the TikTok video. "It's slow today." He grumbled. "She didn't come in." He referred to their boss. "Something came up with one of her kids." Alexis' nervous system relaxed to average speed. She washed up and started her usual duties.

Customers trickled in throughout the day. Alexis rechecked her phone, but still no response. It was time for her first break. She stepped outside the back of the restaurant and called him. It went straight to voicemail. Alexis sighed, ending the call without leaving a message.

She walked back in and sat down to grab a quick bite. She still had a few minutes before getting back on the clock. The solemn waitress scrolled her social media. None of the posts interested her. A small crowd entered, settling in. She took a final sip before tossing the cup in the trash. She popped a gum in her mouth before taking their drink orders. The group was water and tea fans. She stepped away to fill their drinks, giving them time to review the menu. She looked over at the empty bench where he would sit and sent another message, adding a kissy face emoji. Alexis carried the tray of drinks to the animated group; their day was going better than hers. Wings, fries, and seafood platters were the meals of choice. She handed the order to the cook and started wiping down the empty tables, counting the minutes until her shift ended.

It rained on and off, causing Alexis to keep adjusting her wipers. She thought about her grocery stock, as she passed up a store. It was going to be a light homemade sandwich and chips for dinner. She reached for her cell phone again while stopped at a light and had no notifications. She dropped it in the cup holder before the light turned green.

She removed her wet jacket and shook her damp braids loose when she got home. She tossed her purse on the sofa and turned on the TV to click through streaming options when the dead image of Brienne popped into her head. The horrible vision reminded her that she still had the woman's cell. She didn't want to face the questions the police would ask if she turned it in now. As she flipped through new episodes on Hulu, she remembered that in her high, drunken stupor, she told her one-night stand about the dead woman's phone. She retrieved the box from the coat closet and removed the lid. The phone was gone.

"Damn it!" She shouted before throwing herself down the sofa, covering her face. "Why would he take it?" She screamed into her palms, kicking her legs in the air.

Alexis put the joint between her lips. A plate with a few remaining chips was on the sofa near her feet. She thought about the green coin she found in the woman's wallet, the one with the name Haven in the center. She got her laptop and opened the web browser.

CHAPTER 19

CHELSEA

When I called, my father was going to a doctor's appointment. He had some health issues due to excessive drinking, a habit that progressively got worse after he and my mother split.

"Aww, get out the way!" He shouted at the traffic. "Can't we get around this?" He asked his girlfriend who was behind the wheel. When I first met Gayle, I thought she was clingy, noticing the decrease in solo visits from my father.

"You're a grumpy one this morning," I said.

"No, sorry, love. I gotta be on time for this appointment." He apologized.

"That's your daughter?" Gayle questioned.

"Mais, yeah. Look, turn here!" He commanded Gayle. "Get out of this mess." A quick pause. "I've been watching the news." He spoke to me.

"Yeah. I'm glad the media didn't make Haven the focus of the story."

"Okay, well, I guess that's a good thing. I just wanted to check on my baby girl."

"Thanks, I appreciate it."

"You know I'm here if you need me. I rarely hear from you and your sister these days."

"I've just been busy with everything. I'm short-staffed at the moment."

"Oh, okay, I understand now. No hard feelings, then." Gayle said something about finding a good parking spot. "Look, we just pulled up to the doctor's office."

"Okay, later, talk soon."

"Talk soon. Have a good day."

Staff moved around the office in a busy bee fashion, taking calls, entering data, and scanning documents. It was early November, and the holidays were soon approaching. It was the time of year when donors tended to be more generous, and companies picked charities for end-of-the-year write-offs. So far, the funds we received sustained our operations, but nowhere near prior years.

The new hire, Franklin Johnson, walked past my office, popping his head in to say hello.

"I'm a little early for my onboarding today, but I wanted to make a stop." He showed me the pastry box in his hand.

"I already had a scone." I patted my stomach. "They look delicious, though."

"I'll make sure to save you one for later." He smiled, going back into the hallway.

Franklin was settling in nicely. He had a way of getting people to warm up. My cell rang. It was Damien Brown. I prayed he had good news.

"Hey, Chelsea!"

"Hey Damien, how's it going?"

"Good, I have some great news for you."

I threw praised hands in the air. "I could use some. Please tell."

"Remember the potential donor I mentioned the other day?"

"Oh, yes, the doctor with the clinic."

"I spoke to him today, and he wants to donate."

"Really?!" I shouted, getting the attention of nearby staff. I got up to close my door. "How much?"

"Twenty thousand dollars for his initial donation."

"What? That's more than I expected. So, he wants to continue donating?

"Yes, he hinted at making it an annual gift."

"That's what I'm talking about." I clapped my hands and spun around in the chair. "I'll have to offer you a job soon."

"Oh, no. I'm good. Like I said before, it's not about money for me."

"I know, but I'm just saying. Your performance is surpassing our community managers."

"I appreciate the compliment. Whatever I can do to help."

We agreed to meet soon and discuss our new donor and other prospects Damien had. The miracle message he just delivered put a smile on my face that lasted long past the end of our conversation. I had to share the news with someone. My first instinct was to head toward Marsha's office, but then I remembered she wasn't there. She texted me a few days ago, testing the water. Her daughter was in town, and she was happy to spend time with her.

My cell phone dinged. It was Iman. I hadn't called her like I promised. I needed to contact some other potential partners, or Damien would soon be running Haven. I called her, planning for a quick check-in.

"I updated my online dating profile." Iman huffed. "Sean and I have been together for two months, and no mention of marriage, a family."

"Well-" I began.

"When I brought it up," she cut me off, "he looked at me like I was crazy, and I haven't heard from him in a few days."

"But Iman, it hasn't been that long; give it some time." I opened my office door and headed to the break room.

"You think?" She considered.

"Yes," I emphasized. I filled my tumbler with ice, smiling at one of the community managers, and she popped in to put a lunch tote in the refrigerator.

"I'm just confused. How do you ask me if I have kids or have been married, yada yada, in one of our initial conversations, but when I ask those same things regarding us, you go cold?"

"I understand." My friend made a point. I filled my container halfway with water and mixed in some Powerade. "Maybe it scared him." I lowered my tone, exiting the break room. "It's still early. Y'all need to get to know each other more."

"I guess." She thought it over.

"Well, I've been seeing someone." I closed my office door behind me.

"Oh, you've been keeping a secret." She accused me like when we were kids.

"I wanted to wait." I peeped through the blinds in my office. City workers collected traffic cones off the street.

"Details, please." Iman pleaded.

"His name is Ian, and he's in real estate."

"Last name?"

"Sanchez." I sang into the phone, unlocking my computer.

"Ian Sanchez, huh?" Iman hummed a Latin beat.

"Ha! You have jokes."

"No, I'm happy for you." She giggled. "How long has this been going?"

"A few months now."

"Were you waiting to get a ring before telling your bestie?" Iman teased, but I detected a slight seriousness in her tone.

"No, you're one of only a few people I've told. I wanted to wait and see where it went." I paused. "That's why I think you should be patient with Sean."

"Okay, okay." She whined.

The front door buzzer went off. I stepped out of my office and checked the door camera. The receptionist was out. It was a man I didn't recognize. When he stepped back into view, I saw the logo on his shirt. It was the plumber Grant mentioned when I complained about the office toilets.

"Sorry girl, I have to go. A plumber just got here."

"K, talk soon." She hung up.

I let the plumber in and led him to the bathroom to assess the issue.

I heard my text alert. It was Ian.

Would you like to go to a night market?

Yes! That sounds nice.

Cool. Make sure to bring your appetite.

You know I will. Lol

I want dessert afterward!

I'm always up for something sweet!

CHAPTER 20

SEPTEMBER 1996

Helena got the girls up and ready early so they could eat breakfast at home before she dropped them off at school. She picked up a few things at the grocery store for dinner. Her stomach growled. She skipped the pancakes, eggs, and bacon that she prepared. She tossed a cup of fruit and a juice bottle into her shopping cart.

"Helena!" The pierced call came from the end of the aisle. "Oh my God, it's so good to see you." Mindy Simon's speedy words reached Helena before the tiny-framed woman parallel-parked her basket.

"It's a pleasure to run into you." Helena gripped the handle on her basket, feeling a little light-headed.

"Are you feeling okay?" Mindy stepped closer, reaching out her hand.

"Oh yes," The weak woman waved off her worries. "I just need to eat something."

Mindy snatched the bottle of orange juice and unscrewed the cap before thrusting it at Helena. "Drink some. It'll help." She reached into her cart and opened a container of croissants, handing one over.

Helena took a bite of the buttered bread before swallowing some juice.

"I do it all the time when Erika's sugar gets low."

"Thank you." Helena took another bite. "It's starting to work."

"Good." Mindy smiled. "Does this happen off?"

"No." Helena straightened her back. "I made a big breakfast for the girls but didn't feel like eating, and then it hit me suddenly.

"That's a mom for you." Mindy preached. "Sometimes we forget to take care of ourselves."

"I know. That's why I'm here." Helena looked around the pasta section. "I'm trying to decide what to cook for dinner."

Mindy tapped her fingers on the cart. "Why don't we both take a break one day this week and take our girls out for dinner?"

"That sounds nice, but I have so much to do at home, and they have so much homework."

"We won't stay out too late." Mindy insisted. "It'll be my treat. Erika and Chelsea would love it."

"Uhm, yes, they would." Helena thought it over. "Okay, sure."

Mindy moved in for an energetic hug. They wrapped up their shopping and rolled their carts toward checkout.

Helena pulled into the thrift store donation lane. A worker stepped through automatic sliding doors as she popped open the trunk. He hauled her bags inside the center before returning to the car.

"Do you need a receipt?" he asked.

"No, that's okay."

"Okay, thanks for the donation, ma'am."

Helena drove off the lot and headed back to the house. She sat at the dining room table, staring at the prescription bottle of pills. She hated taking them, but the capsules made the stress go away long enough until her next dose. The school year had recently begun, and she had the house to herself during the day. Charla and Chelsea were getting older with developing social lives. Even when they were home, she looked for things to pass the time. She missed meeting up with the Ladies in Service Society women, but lately, she wasn't in the mood to socialize. The mother of two opened the Word document on her laptop. Her resume needed refreshing. She was a high school teacher when she got pregnant with Charla. Charles didn't want his pregnant wife to work. At the time, she welcomed staying at home, letting her successful life insurance agent for a husband lead as sole provider. Selene suggested substitute teaching to get her feet wet again, saying the classroom wasn't the same. Helena pulled up the Lafayette Parish School board website and began to search.

Glow-in-the-dark stars covered the wall, except for the designated spaces featuring posters of music groups Immature and TLC. The clear phone sat propped against the young teenager's leg. Charla sat on the bed, with the mirror in hand, carefully applying brown lip liner and light pink gloss. Chelsea sat on a bean bag chair on the other side of the room, leaning over, chin in her palms, gawking at her sister.

"That's your fifth time putting that stuff on today." Chelsea rolled her eyes.

"You're just jealous because you don't know anything about makeup."

"Whatever, that's why you can't wear it outside the house." She returned to writing in her diary, twirling the troll pencil as she thought about her next sentence.

"Those things are creepy." Charla side-eyed the stout creature with its wild, bright yellow hair.

"So, I like them. Give me your phone." Chelsea held her hand out, waiting for her sister to comply. Charla handed it over. "Why did you want a see-through one anyway?" Her younger sister played with the receiver.

"It's transparent." Charla corrected.

"Same thing."

"Don't keep it off the hook like that."

"Waiting on a call or something?" Chelsea put it down.

Charla ignored the question and took out some eyeshadow.

"You think you're so grown." Her younger sister stuck out her tongue. "You still have a pillow person." Chelsea pointed toward the top shelf in the open closet.

"It'll be vintage when I'm older, and I can sell it for more money," Charla said confidently. Chelsea mimicked her sister's words, snapping her head from side to side before turning to a blank page in her diary. "What are you writing about? It's not like you have a boyfriend."

"Mom and Dad said you can't have a boyfriend yet, either." Chelsea snapped back, then remembered their father wasn't in the house to enforce that rule.

"I'm in high school now." The young teen rolled her head and straightened her neck, admiring her framed glossy lips, puckering up to the mirror. "It's not my fault you're still in middle school."

"Ugh." Chelsea let the open journal fall on her face. Their mother called from downstairs; it was time for dinner. Chelsea made it out of the room first. Charla put the makeup back in her purple and teal caboodle and slid it far under the bed.

When they got downstairs, they set the table while Helena positioned the meal in the center. Chelsea sniffed as their mother uncovered the dishes: roast beef, rice and gravy, sweet peas, and potato salad. "What's this?" she asked, holding up her mother's pills.

"It's nothing. I left it on the table." Helena took the bottle and slid it into her pocket.

They said grace and started to load their plates. The phone rang. Chelsea got up to answer it. It was their father.

"He knows it's dinnertime," Helena muttered under her breath. "Ask if you can call him back after we eat."

Chelsea delivered her mother's request. She listened to his rebuttal. "He said he can't talk later, so that's why he's calling now."

"Well, tell him it will have to wait until tomorrow when he's not too busy to speak to his children." Helena's voice climbed.

Charles heard every word. His daughter reluctantly relayed his reply. "He said calling at dinnertime is not a crime, and he has the right to call his own house at whatever time he wants."

"Let him know this is my house, too, and if he wants to speak to you, he can do it at an appropriate time!" Helena slammed her fist on the table; her piercing tone shot up to the ceiling, threatening to shake the chandelier. Chelsea put down the phone, tears falling down her cheeks, and sat back at the table. Charla reached under the table to hold her sister's hand. Helena never got up, leaving the phone off the hook and their father's mousy voice shouting back on the other end. Their mother straightened the napkin on her lap before picking up her fork to enjoy her meal. She motioned to her children to do the same. That evening, the dining room was void of talks about their school day, new friends they met, or if there was a cute boy in class. The only sounds were the clanging of silverware, slow, attentive chewing, and cautious sips.

CHAPTER 21

NOVEMBER 2023

CHAD

I sat at the bistro table on my balcony. I bit into the chicken salad sandwich and popped a few sea salt and black pepper chips in my mouth. The neighbor in the unit below me walked to her car, waving before she got in. I returned the greeting with a quick hand flip and returned my attention to Brienne's phone. A call illuminated my cell's screen. It was the girl from the restaurant. I let it go to voicemail. I examined the glass screen protector and luxury case. Brienne's wallpaper was a candid shot of her in a sea green knit tank top and jeans, leaning forward, hands on her hips, captured in mid-laughter. She liked using dates for passwords, a bit of information she shared during one of our late-night chats. I tried her birthday and the date her father died. She wore a necklace with the numbers representing the day she got saved, but that didn't work either. Then I remembered the date she checked into Haven. The reinvented woman revealed her battle with addiction to me over time. I learned she had gotten close to my younger half-sister, Chelsea, during her stint at the center.

I scanned her text messages and saw she hadn't deleted our thread. There were conversations with other men and group chats flooded with silly GIFs. I switched to the image gallery. I skipped past the recent ones before landing on the photos that predated her recovery.

Brienne used to be a hooker, but she preferred escort. It was a formal touch to the age-old profession, a term you might use if legally obligated to report income on a tax return.

"I know people still judge me because of it." She said one evening, burying her face in the sheets.

"Everyone has a past, love," I told her, tracing my finger along her spine and between her plump cheeks.

"I appreciate that." She lifted her head, pulling a pillow under her chin. "It's not easy to talk about it." A tear slid down her cheek.

"I'll never judge you," I assured.

She considered my words before rolling over to kiss me.

The first set of explicit photos popped up. They showed a scantily clad Brienne in bed with mostly older men. She disclosed the names of some clients and their professions to me. They included judges, attorneys, doctors, and politicians. I skimmed through more images and videos, admiring the fearlessness in her crafty, devious smile. The cunning female wasn't catching feelings back then. I slid open the balcony door. I got a Red Bull and settled at the dining table. I took the burner phone out of the bag.

I put on my favorite pair of Asics running shoes and filled my bottle with ice water before darting out the door. The cool breeze was a welcomed change from the summer's three-digit degree heat. As I ran along the park's path, I smiled at parents feeding ducks with their kids or pushing them on the swings. A couple lay on a blanket with a basket between them, holding hands as they looked up at the sky. The call came through my Air Pods. It was Yvette. Shit. Not today.

"Hello. I just sent money for rent and to fix the a/c."

"Hello, ya-self. That's how you greet your mom."

"I'm in the middle of a run." I slowed down my pace and started to walk, pulling the water bottle from my vest pocket.

"Oh, sorry. I wanted to know if you had Thanksgiving plans."

I took a long gulp. Getting paid, I thought; words I heard many times as a kid. "No, I don't."

"You wanna spend it with me? I can cook your favorites."

"I'm traveling for work the following week, and I have a lot to do before I leave."

"K, I see." She banged a pot in the sink before turning on the faucet. "Just thought I'd offer." She tossed more dishes in the water.

"I'll see what I can do."

"It would be nice to see you." Her voice was solemn. "The last time I saw you, I hardly recognized you. You changed so much over the years."

"We've been over this."

"I don't know why you cover your light eyes with those damn contacts. I thought that's what people wanted, and your hair is so different now-"

"I should be able to work out something. I'll let you know."

"Well, I ain't goin' keep you. Don't seem like you want to talk anyway." She paused. "Love, you."

"Okay, you, too."

After hanging up with Yvette, I put my cell on Do Not Disturb before dropping it and my earpieces in the other pocket. I ran harder, pounding the ground beneath me. The park became dull. The sight of others engaging in outdoor activities no longer interested me.

CHAPTER 22

CHARLA

"I think you're reading too much into it. Mom could have been anywhere, Charla." Chelsea ruffled through drawers in her bathroom.

"She told me she was at home, and you know she keeps that air purifier and the television on at night. I didn't hear either of those."

"Maybe she wants to keep it private for now." My sister defended.

"Like you do with your boyfriend, Ian?" I teased.

"Whatever, cher. You've met Ian before."

"Yes, but it's been a minute. What does he look like again?"

"Olive or Avocado Oil?" My sister was in the middle of an oil treatment.

"Both. That's fine if our mom wants to keep her relations to herself. I'm just happy she's seeing someone."

"We don't know that yet. Ahh! One sec, some oil got in my eyes." She ran the water and slammed a door shut. "Don't you have a date tonight with your friend?"

"Yes, I do, and you know his name is Preston."

"I don't want to make you late."

"No, you're fine. We're just hanging out tonight."

"That's all y'all are doing?" She questioned, turning on the hair dryer.

"Yep." I flung open the doors to my closet.

"And you want to talk about mom." She chastised. "How's Travis?" Do y'all still keep in touch?"

"Yeah, we do." I paused. "He asked about you the other day."

"That's nice of him. I always liked him." The dryer hummed, attempting to drown out her words. "Can you hear me, okay?"

"Yeah, your voice is just low." I held up a dress next to a jumper.

"I don't know why you two never got together."

"Because we are just friends, that's why," I stressed. "Now, I have to go."

"Oh, thought you had time. Did I hit a nerve?"

"Bye, cher. Talk soon. Love ya."

I freshened up and slipped into a low-cut, sheer black bodycon dress with heels. Preston arrived on time with flowers and a box of gourmet treats from a cookie place I liked. I planted a long kiss on his moist lips.

After rushing my sister off the phone, I prepared a quick meal: pasta and meatballs with a side salad.

"This is delicious. I knew you could cook." Preston smiled, chewing on a mouthful of beef and pasta.

"Thanks, but wait until you taste my other dishes." I bragged.

"Sounds promising." He drank some peach green tea. "Where is your daughter?"

"With her father." I leaned in to give him another kiss, licking tea remnants off my lips. Preston's eyes lit up as he took a closer view of my dress. I waited for the assault.

He released his lips from mine and dug in for another bite. "There's a good show on Netflix we can check out."

"Okay." I threw myself against the back of the chair, pushing my partially eaten plate away.

"I guess you're not hungry."

"Not for this." I sighed.

I sat next to him as we settled in on the sofa. I took the remote out of the end table drawer and handed it over before taking out my cell phone. He slid his hand over mine and put my cell in the drawer. He kissed my neck softly before selecting a show. I waited a few minutes after the episode started before sliding my hand up his thigh, towards his zipper, but he jerked backward. I snatched the remote and paused the actors on the screen.

"Something wrong?" He asked.

"Yeah." I snapped.

"Do you want me?"

He sat up, clearing his throat, reaching for my hand again. "Of course I do; look at you," he gestured his hand at my body. "You're beautiful and smart."

"So, what is it then? All we do is kiss." I got up from the couch.

"Don't take it the wrong way. I'm not one to rush into anything."

"I understand, but some reassurance that you want to at some point would be nice."

"I do, just—" He made me wait while he chose his words carefully. I swayed back and forth. "Not before marriage."

"What?!" I exclaimed.

"I practice celibacy."

"I don't know what to say." I sat back on the opposite end of the sofa, tugged my dress down, and crossed my legs.

"I haven't always been this way," Preston explained. "I used to be the complete opposite."

"Oh, really." I sulked.

"We have a group on social media." He pressed on.

"A group?" I questioned.

"It's like a support system." He rapidly tapped his fingers on his knees. "It's not easy to hold out nowadays."

"Okay." I looked away. "I respect you for doing that."

"Are you okay with holding out until marriage?" He moved closer, putting his arms around me.

"I mean, I have a daughter, so I'm not the definition of celibate."

"We believe that you can start at any time."

"I'm older than you. Do you want children?"

"Yes."

"I know there are ways-" I began.

"Plus, I'm okay with a stepchild if we're unable to have children." Preston cut in.

"I don't think you've thought this through. You have plenty of time to decide."

"I have thought about it." He reiterated. "I hoped we could be on the same page."

"This is just a shock." I pulled away. "I wish I would have known about this sooner."

"Of course, I don't expect you to decide tonight."

"No, of course not." I hit play on the remote and dropped it on the sofa between us. No wonder Preston was a dating perfectionist. He had to be before dropping a bomb like this.

CHAPTER 23

DECEMBER 1996

It was Christmas Eve, and the sisters were huddled next to each other on a beat-up couch in front of a television with no cable at their grandmother's house in Grand Coteau, a small town in St. Landry Parish. The old wooden house was packed with family the sisters hadn't seen in a long time; their younger cousins chased each other, slamming the screen door, while the adults stood around in the cramped kitchen drinking their holiday spirit of choice, sneaking seconds from open food trays. The smell of roux escaped the tall pot of gumbo every time someone lifted the lid. Charla and Chelsea watched as their uncle, their Dad's older brother, slapped him on the back, holding a flask in his other hand, laughing and snorting at a joke from when they were kids. Once the chuckles simmered down, he walked over to his daughters, leaving his kin to continue without him.

"Why aren't y'all talking with your family, playing with your cousins?" He gestured with an unsteady wave.

"They're smaller than us." Charla pushed her fists deep into the sofa, defending her position of isolation.

"Yeah, I don't know them." Chelsea pouted, resting her chin on the arm of the couch.

"How do you expect to know them if you don't speak?" Charles took another sip from his glass.

Charla turned her head towards the others, offering a forced grin, while Chelsea shrugged her shoulders before burying her head in a cushion.

"Why don' you take 'em to see da lights, Charlie?" Their grandmother's raspy voice entered the living room. The older woman lowered her body into a rocking chair, placing a pack of cigarettes on the arm. "Dey not used to us, cher. You and dat wife of yours didn' bring 'em round 'nough." She moved her worn, wrinkled hand to slip a cigarette from the pack, looking around for her lighter. Chelsea spotted it on the other side of the TV stand.

"You see my lighter, chile?"

"No, ma'am," Chelsea replied, looking away.

"That's not it by the t.v.?" Her grandmother squinted.

"Yes," Chelsea nodded reluctantly.

"Get it fa me, cher." Her elder commanded. Her granddaughter dragged herself over to the entertainment center to retrieve it. "Mais cher, I don' bite!" She snapped as Chelsea handed it over.

"Can we go see the lights now, Dad?" Chelsea pleaded.

"Fine, let's go." Their father barked.

Chelsea hugged her grandmother, waving away the cigarette smoke. Charla followed with a side hug, towering over the small, frail woman.

"Y'all have fun, be safe out dere. People crazy around dis time." Their grandmother raised her thin arm, waving them off as the screen door slammed behind them.

139

"Y'all embarrassed me, you know that, right?" Charles chastised as they settled into the SUV. Neither child spoke. "Y'all don't act like this around your momma's family." They drove off the front lawn and down a long, dusty road.

"I can't wait to see the lights!" Chelsea perked up as their father approached the highway, heading back to Lafayette.

Charles maintained a slow pace, still buzzing from the cognac, letting his daughters get the holiday experience each home boasted. "The neighbors on our street put up some huge soldier nutcrackers, too." Chelsea pointed at one of the homes."

"Yeah, that's nice, sweetheart. Look at the one coming up." Her father crawled past the house and onto the next one.

"Enjoying yourself, Charla?" Charles questioned his oldest.

"Yeah, Dad." She whined. "The decorations are pretty."

Their father lowered the window as they approached a family of four standing in the driveway. Their kids handed out hot chocolate with marshmallows while holiday tunes blasted from the garage. "Y'all want some?"

"Yeah, sure." The sisters agreed.

"Thanks, y'all. Merry Christmas and Happy New Year!" Their father accepted three small cups of hot chocolate, white melting squares bobbing above the rim. The parents loaded the trays with more cups before sending their kids to the next vehicle in line. Charles turned the corner and crept down the next row of sparkling homes.

      Christmas day was usually at their family home. Their mother soldiered through the house, adjusting the garland on the stair railing, ornaments, and lights that shifted on the tree, obsessively checking the pots on the stove and the main dish in the oven. Their father retreated to the office, busying himself and filing paperwork until it was time to eat.

      Helena entered the fine dining restaurant with her daughters, parents, and Selene with her husband and son in tow. She wore a black evening dress with a matching long-sleeved black and gold velvet jacket. Helena sat at the table, head and shoulders held high, prepared to enjoy a meal with her loved ones.

      "Where ole' Charlie, Helena?" Her mother sat across from her, next to her father. Helena hesitated at the mention of her husband's name.

      "He's not coming, cher, remember?" Helena's father nudged his wife. "They're not together." He whispered.

      Helena smiled at her father and turned to her mother. "That's right, ma. Remember we talked about that."

      Her mother shook her head and waved off her forgetfulness. "I remember him and his lil' nappy head coming to da house chasin' after you when y'all was kids. Mais la…" Her voice trailed off as something got her attention.

      "Does everyone know what they want to order?" Selene shifted gears, looking around for the waiter. Her husband picked up his menu again, double-checking his selection. "You never could make up your mind." She said, a hint of tension in her voice. He grunted as he examined the entrées again.

Grant tugged at the tight collar on his shirt and loosened his tie, earning a daring look from Selene. He smacked the large green bow on his cousin Chelsea's red and green plaid skirt. "I know what you took out of my room." His cousin covered her mouth. "I'll get you back."

"If you do, I'll tell." Chelsea threatened a quick toss of her head toward his parents.

"Y'all are so immature." Charla sat proudly across the table in a dark green high-neck velvet dress, rolling her eyes. Her sister and cousin responded with twisted faces, tongues sticking out.

"Y'all better behave down there." A harsh whispered command from Selene flowed down the table toward them.

The waiter came over with a basket of fresh hot bread and butter. He apologized for the slow service; they were swamped tonight for the holiday. He started with the elderly couple, working with Selene to get their order, and then continued around the table. Charla noticed her mother as the waiter's voice drowned in the background, taking selections from Grant and Chelsea. Helena sat in a daze, staring at the Italian art on the wall behind them. She smiled at her daughter before getting up from the table and asking the waiter about the bathroom. Charla got up, but Helena raised her hand, stopping her daughter.

"No, stay at the table." She ordered Charla. "I'll be right back."

CHAPTER 24

CHAD

I sat on Aunt Lyn's living room floor, flipping through the television channels. Her kids were still ripping through the Christmas wrapping paper and kicking boxes around. The baby was crying in the back room.

"Go see about her, Jimmy." She shoved her husband out of the recliner.

Yvette cuddled up on the sofa with a guy she met in an online chat room a few months ago. She kept bragging to my aunt that her new friend drove out of state to spend time with her on Christmas. He was short and skinny, with a pointy nose and beady eyes.

"Enjoying yourself, son?" He patted me on the head.

"You're not my father." I brushed his hand away.

"Be polite, Chadwick," Yvette said, rubbing his knee.

"Where is his father?" Her boyfriend asked.

"Out of state, but he's not in the picture." My mother assured, taking his hand in her lap.

"He's with his family in Louisiana," I said. "We're not allowed to see them again." The man sat back, looking a bit uneasy.

"Chad!" Yvette's voice rose. Go play with your cousins."

"That's what I read on the paper." I tugged on an ornament dangling from the five-foot tree.

"Right now!" She ordered.

I joined in the destroying of wrapping paper. I thought about how nice my father's big house probably looked, with lights and animated decorations like in the wealthy neighborhoods. My sisters are probably smiling, jumping around with expensive gifts, and calling up their friends to say what they got for Christmas. My mom kept her promise and bought me a new pair of Nike Air Max. The sprinter Michael Johnson wore them at the Olympics in Atlanta. I also got clothes, a truck from my aunt, and some cash from my grandparents. I kept my box of new shoes out of sight, not wanting my relatives to mess them up.

"Who wants cake? We got red velvet, and I baked some brownies." Aunt Lyn yelled from the kitchen. Her kids trampled over me, breaking their necks to get the first bite. I got up and waited for my aunt to hand me a small plate of dessert after serving the rowdy bunch. My mother was still in the living room, whispering something in the ear of her elf-looking friend.

"Can you bring us some cake, baby?" She called after me.

"Okay." I didn't turn around to face them. I was busy counting the years I had left until I could break free, away from this place.

Aunt Lyn dropped a heavy slice of cake and a chunk of brownie on my plate. "Sit at the table and eat sweetie."

"But my mom asked to get them some."

"Her man has two legs of his own, don't he?" She questioned aloud as she put aside two pieces of cake.

My mom's boyfriend took the slices and forks. "We're going to get some fresh air." He said as my mother followed him out the door.

Aunt Lyn's husband returned to the front room, holding the wet-faced baby. "Y'all eating dessert without me?"

"You're nothing but a big kid." My aunt handed him a plate, taking her baby girl in her arms and kissing her cheeks.

"Don't grow up to be like him, "she said, leaning back on the sofa, "or like them men your momma brings around. She thrusted her thumb at Yvette and her boyfriend's dark figures in the window.

"That's none of our business, Evelyn." Her husband munched on a large chunk of brownie.

"She's my sister, and he's my nephew. It is my business." Aunt Lyn snapped, scaring the baby. "Oh, Lawd." She stood up to rock her from side to side.

"Go get her blankie in the crib, please."

I hurried down the hall and returned with my baby cousin's pink and white blanket.

"You listen to what I said, Chad." Aunt Lyn stressed. "I know what I'm talking about."

"Yes, ma'am."

Uncle Jimmy turned up his Boyz II Men Christmas album. "Leeet it snow…" he botched the song, dancing in the living room, coaxing Aunt Lyn to join him.

145

"You see, I got this baby." She shooed him away.

He handed the infant to me and pulled his wife close, putting his arms around her waist. My little cousin's innocent eyes studied me before she bit my nose.

"Ow!" I held her at arm's length. "She bit me."

"She's just trying to kiss you." Aunt Lyn teased.

The baby girl giggled. My aunt and her husband continued dancing while my cousins pointed and laughed. My arms ached, so I held my cousin against my chest. She rested her head on my shoulder before falling asleep.

CHAPTER 25

NOVEMBER 2023

CHELSEA

Ian left a voicemail asking if we could have an early Thanksgiving meal before spending time with our families. He hinted that he wanted to talk about something. I was about to call him back when, Tanisha Edmond, the new assistant, arrived early, putting her things down at Marsha's old desk and taking her lunch bag to the break room. I recently processed Marsha out, ending her time at Haven.

"That was the only time I ever took money from the center." Her teary eyes explained over the computer screen. "I promise I paid back every dime."

"I appreciate you reconciling what was taken," I said.

"I've never done anything like that before." Marsha hung her head down. "I'll never forgive myself."

"I mailed your belongings, so they should be delivered any day now."

"Thank you, Ms. Chelsea." She wiped her eyes with a tissue.

After Khristian Babineaux left early for an emergency, Tanisha entered my office.

"Do you have a minute to review this new application?"

"Sure, what's it for?" I asked.

"The clerical position." Tanisha placed the CV and cover letter on my desk. She lingered at the doorway.

"Do you have something else for me?"

"No, it was just the application stuff." She leaned against the door frame. "Ms. Richard." She began.

"Yes?"

"I was reviewing some of the documents your previous assistant created. I merged a lot of them to cut down on the files."

"Oh, okay, thanks. I appreciate you doing that."

"It's just that I recognized a couple of the donors on the list." She stepped back inside and sat down.

"Okay." I looked up from the documents.

"They gave a large sum of money and then nothing."

"Sometimes that happens; donors can be very generous one year for whatever reason and go silent the next."

"I know, I understand that. I worked for another nonprofit before. I was just shocked, is all." Tanisha emphasized. "I hounded them for a long time at my last position."

"I see, but like I said, sometimes we just can't case these donors and how they pick their charities." My office phone rang. "Let me take this."

Tanisha nodded in agreement and excused herself.

"Haven recovery center," I answered.

"Hello. I asked to speak to someone in charge, and they transferred me." The shaky female voice said.

"Hi, yes, this is Chelsea. How can I help you?" I heard deep, uneasy breathing. I wondered if it was someone who might need to speak with one of our counselors through the helpline.

"I think I know the person who might have hurt that girl." The woman spoke up abruptly.

"Wait, what do you mean?"

"That dead girl on the news, the one found in the park."

"Oh!" I got up to shut my office door and hurried back to my desk. "You know something about what happened to Brienne?"

"I know a guy who might be connected to her."

"Go on." I encouraged. She went silent. "Are you still there?"

"Yeah, sorry." She said after a moment. "I was in the park that day. I saw her body." Her voice cracked. "I was looking around in the car because it looked weird that someone left it unlocked."

"Okay." I put my hand on my leg to stop it from shaking.

"I didn't mean to take the phone. I forgot I had it in my purse." The woman rambled. "After I saw the woman sitting up like that against the tree, I almost passed out."

"Wait, you have her cell phone?" I searched my cell for the police officer's contact information.

"I don't have it anymore. That's why I'm calling. He took it."

I ceased searching. "Who took it?"

"The dude I was talking to. I know he took it. I couldn't figure out why and remembered I found a green medallion with your center's name on it."

"Sounds like one of our center's sobriety chips," I said. "Did you take anything else?"

"No, ma'am. Of course not." The anonymous caller went silent again.

"What's his name?"

"I looked around on your website and saw his picture, but it was a different name than the one he gave me." Her voice went in and out.

"What name did he give you?"

"He talked about -web designer - going back to school-business courses - starting a business and stuff." She went on talking as if she never heard me. The woman was either moving around, or the connection was terrible, but I understood most of what she said. "-knew people with money-lies!" she bawled.

"What's his name?" I demanded. I wanted to reach my hands through the phone and grab the woman by the shoulders, forcing her to give it up. The call dropped. I frantically checked the caller ID on the office phone, but she blocked the number. "No!" I yelled. I thought about what the woman said about the guy being on our website.

"Tanisha!" I rushed out of my office and busted in on Tanisha, causing her to jump in her seat and almost knocking over her computer monitor.

150

"Yes, ma'am?" She questioned, resembling a deer in headlights.

"Those large donations you asked me about. Can you pull them up again?"

"Yes, of course." The diligent assistant pulled the charts for me with just a few clicks of her wireless mouse. She turned the screen toward me. The same board member secured the sponsorship donations Tanisha highlighted. It was Damien Brown.

"Thank you so much! Please email that to me now."

"Okay, certainly." She opened her inbox to compose a message.

"I need to leave. If anyone needs to reach me, refer them to my cell."

"Okay, will do."

I grabbed my handbag and car fob. I called Damien Brown's number. It went straight to voicemail. I threw my bags on the car's passenger seat and called Charla's number from the car dashboard media screen. She didn't pick up. I sped off the center's parking lot and onto the road. There was a loud honk from an oncoming truck that swerved into the next lane. A call came through.

"Charla!" I screamed.

"Hello, Ms. Richard." The deep male voice was certainly not my sister.

"Who is this?" I asked.

"This is Andre Tyler from KPAL. I'm calling to ask if you would like to respond to recent allegations and documents sent to our station accusing Haven of blackmailing donors into paying for sponsorships."

"What?!" I slammed on the brakes, just missing hitting the car in front of me.

"The documents and pictures allege that the late Brienne Landrieu, a former patient of Haven, worked as an escort, and many of your major donors were her clients."

"Haven would never be a part of some shit like that!" I shouted.

"Is that your official response?" asked the prick reporter.

"No! I have no further comments." I disconnected the call.

I called Charla again, screaming at the media screen for her to answer.

CHAPTER 26

CHARLA

I loaded the dishwasher while scrolling through social media, looking for the celibacy groups Preston mentioned. He left me several messages since our last evening together. I ignored his latest call when I was out with Travis.

"Is everything okay?" Travis asked when my phone kept going off at the table.

"Yes, it's fine." I silenced it before putting it down on the seat. "I like this." I pointed toward the stage at the band.

"I knew you would." He smiled. "This bar always has good music."

"We'll have to come again, then." I lifted my cocktail.

"You know I'm down." Travis clinked his liquor against mine.

My sister called again, interrupting my trolling. I left it ring a few times before picking it up. "What is it now?" I asked out loud before accepting the call.

"I just wanted to ask if I could have more juice." Dede's school was closed because they lost power in last night's storm. "Did I do something wrong?"

"Hold on, Chelsea." I wiped my hands dry on a dish towel and hugged my daughter. "No, sweetie, Mommy was talking out loud. Take whichever one you want." She grabbed the orange mango.

"Why weren't you picking up the phone?! My sister shouted.

"Dede, go in your room while I speak to your Aunt Chell." My daughter skipped back down the hall to her room, bottle in hand. "Uhm, I have a life, you know. I can't answer all the time. What's your problem?" I snapped.

"I got a call from a woman saying she knew who did something to Brienne."

"What?!" I dropped a plate on the floor.

"Yeah, the caller told me all this stuff about how she took Brienne's cell by accident, and a guy she was seeing stole it."

"That's crazy." I examined the plate for cracks. "Do you believe this woman?"

"Wait, there's more." Chelsea took a deep breath. "She looked on Haven's website and saw a picture of the dude. She said he gave her a different name."

"Are you serious?" I slammed the dishwasher closed and started the wash.

"Yes! Tanisha, the new hire, told me she was suspicious about some donations in our records."

"What suspicious amounts?" I wondered why I never caught it.

"Some large amounts from donors she couldn't get at her last job."

"I don't understand. Why is that suspicious?"

"I explained all that to her, but that's not the point!" Chelsea's voice rose again. "Guess who is tied to the donations?"

"Who?"

"Damien Brown!"

"Not him, huh?" I tried processing the puzzle pieces my sister tossed on the table. "What does all this mean?"

"A reporter called me." Chelsea's voice split before heavy sobs almost took her breath away. "Haven is being accused of blackmailing donors to give sponsorships."

"Where the hell did that come from?!"

"The media received proof that Brienne was an escort, and some of our donors were her clients."

"I'll be damned." My sister cried uncontrollably. "Chell, calm down. We will fight this. No one will believe that."

"Yeah, but you know how people talk. It doesn't matter if it's true. Haven is over!" She exclaimed.

"No, it's not. I won't let you give up. Did you call Damien?"

"Yes, and of course, he's not answering."

"Bastard. Did the woman say anything else?"

"The connection was bad before the call dropped, but I remember she said something about him telling her he was taking business classes so he could start a company."

When my sister mentioned the business courses, I put her on hold and called our mother.

I clicked back over. "I think she is teaching a class right now."

"Try again," Chelsea pleaded.

"Hey, sweetie, I'm in the middle of class. Is something wrong?"

"Yes, ma, do you have a minute?"

"Everything is wrong!" Chelsea cut in.

"Chell? I thought Charla called me."

"I did. I merged the call."

"What's going on? Y'all have me worried." Her voice echoed.

Chelsea repeated what she had just told me, adding more details as she went along.

"Who did this?" Our mother demanded.

"Damien Brown, one of our board members," I replied, letting my sister catch her breath. "He's taking some business courses at the university; that's why I called you."

"He's a student," our mother whispered. "One day, he came to class and his eyes were different. I thought he looked familiar, but I brushed it off. It's been almost thirty years."

"What are you talking about, Mom?" Chelsea exclaimed. "You're not making sense!"

"I have to go."

"Mom, don't hang up!" I commanded, but she hung up.

Dede was back in the kitchen, standing close behind me. "Go back in your room. I'll come in a minute."

"I don't want to." She frowned. "What's wrong?"

"This is grown-up business," I explained, pointing down the hall.

"I'm in your driveway," Chelsea said, slamming her car door.

CHAPTER 27

CHAD

Seated in the darkened lecture room of the business night class, I watched as the steel-spined bitch reviewed the information on the slides, glancing back at the screen at all the appropriate times. Helena Richard was a good professor. I was surprised that she kept her married name. Professor Richard kept fixing her hair as she clicked through a few more slides. The cell phone screen on the desk brightened up the room again. Helena looked up from the phone at the audience of attentive pupils, scanned the seats, and located her assistant.

"Can you pick up where I left off? I need to take this."

The tall, lanky student wiped his glasses before taking over the presentation. I watched as the professor stepped into the hall. I sat impatiently, half listening to the assistant read through the content on the slides.

"Any questions before I continue?" The teacher's pet asked. No one raised their hand.

Professor Richard walked back in, looking deflated. She found me on the second row from the bottom, on the opposite side of the room. The same fatal glare I remembered as a boy. I imagined she wanted to drag me out of the room, away from the university building, her home away from home.

Helena started walking toward me, fist clenched, but I shoved the laptop in my shoulder bag and slipped out of the room. The wild screams chased me down the hall, ricocheting against the walls.

I ran to the parking lot, aiming my fob at the car to start the engine before throwing my bag inside. When I first moved to Lafayette, I found my father. He no longer lived in the big house downsized to a middle-class home. Alcohol abuse forced Charles Richard, Sr. into retirement. One day, I followed him to a store.

"I prefer The Lawn Mower." I said after lingering in the razor section, keeping my cap down.

"Oh," he stumbled back from the shelf without looking at me. "Where is that one?"

"They don't sell it here. I get it online."

"I don't mess around with all that online shopping." He griped, squinting at the packages, his hand trembling. "I like to get my hands on something before I buy it."

"Understood." I handed him a Gillette from the top shelf. "This is just as good."

"That's the one I usually get." He said proudly. "Thanks, man." He continued down the aisle.

I drove away from the college with its twentieth-century oaks and headed to the north side of town. The neighborhood was modest, with solid homes and clean lawns, but not vain. I parked curbside near the house I watched my father trudge in. I waited before I knocked on the door. A bird-haired, nervous woman answered.

"Can I help you?" She whipped her head.

"Is Charles home?" I asked.

"And who are you?" The door was open just enough for me to see the frame of her body, nothing more.

"I'm Chadwick Celestine. His son." Her eyes widened; her mouth dropped open.

"Uhm," she moved to shut the door, but I forced it open. She ran towards the back of the house, yelling at my father. "Charlie! Come quick."

My father popped into the hallway, squinting as he did so. "Who the hell are you?"

"Your son." I planted my feet in the foyer.

He reached for a pair of glasses on a nearby table. "What-what are you doing here?" He stammered.

"That's all you have to say?"

Charles mumbled, but nothing audible came through.

"It's been a while. Have you tried that razor I suggested?"

He raised his eyebrows. "Gayle." He motioned at the woman perched in the living room. "Go on the other side. Let me handle this."

"But Charlie-" she refused to move.

"Do what I said!" He barked, causing her to jump and abandon her post.

"Now, that's the nigga I remember." I laughed.

"Did your mother put you up to this?"

"Don't worry about my mother. I'm a grown-ass man."

"You're a man, now, huh?" He mocked. "Still acting like a boy that never grew up, I see."

"What would you know about how I grew up?" My mouth foamed.

He moved closer to the sofa. "Look, I know I wasn't there for you like I should have been, but you must understand what I was dealing with." He pleaded his side of the story. "Your mother gave me no choice. She was out of control. I had to protect my family."

"I thought I was family, too."

"You are my son. I never said you weren't. I just." He stopped, his age growing tired of explaining everything. "Look, what is this about? All of that is in the past."

The first time my fist hit my father's face, I didn't even feel it, adrenaline rushing through my veins. He fell against the wall, trying not to hit the floor. Once he regained his composure, he rushed me, forcing us into the living room. We tumbled on the glass-top coffee table. Charles looked over me as he wiped blood from his lip. I felt pieces of glass in my skin and warm liquid running down my arms. I threw another blow that he blocked before attempting to hold down my arms. I spit in his face and shoved him back. I pounced on him, hitting him again in the face before I gripped his neck. My father started gagging, calling out to his woman.

"Charlie!" The parrot flew back in the front room. "I called the police!" She squawked before jumping on my back, wrapping her arms around my neck and her legs around my waist, using her body weight to pull me away from her man. Charles choked, trying to catch his breath. The woman dug her nails in my arms. I reached up and grabbed her head, yanking it to the side.

161

When her grip lightened, I pulled on her arm, throwing her off me. She hit her head on the side of the table that framed the glass. She cried out in agony, grabbing her head. I stood up and backed up into the hall. I thought of Brienne and that day in the park. Chills ran through my body.

"Get your ass out of my house!" Charles yelled. "Don't you ever come back here!"

I left the injured couple and bolted out the front door.

"I know what you've been up to!" Brienne shouted in the car.

"What are you talking about?" I asked, noticing the needle in the center console before she shut the lid.

"Don't play stupid with me!" She jabbed her chest with her finger.

"I don't know what the fuck this is about."

"You used me!" Brienne screamed, biting the inside of her cheek, blood dripping down her lip.

"How did I use you?" I noticed her bloodshot eyes and wild movements. "What did you take?" Brienne leaped out of the car, dodging the question. I got out and went after her. "I thought you were clean."

"This is your fault! You lied to me." She pounded my chest. We had broken up a couple of weeks before going to the park.

"I don't want to be in a committed relationship," I said, petting the head of her Morkie before walking out of the bedroom.

"What?!" She trailed me to the living room, her dog not far behind.

"It's not you. I'm not ready for that now." I explained.

"You called me wifey and talked about having a baby!"

"We were fuckin'! What did you expect me to say?" I paused at the door.

"You piece of shit!" Brienne hollered; her furry companion barked at my heels.

"I'm not husband or father material. Trust me."

"So, why bring it up?!" Brienne stood in the apartment doorway, wiping away tears with her shirt.

"It was in the moment, what you needed to hear at the time," I said calmly.

"Fuck you!" She slammed the door in my face, triggering more yelps from the puppy. I hurried down the stairs.

Brienne moved quickly to a tree away from the parking lot, picking up a branch. "I should have known. All those questions you kept asking about Chelsea and her sister." She drew a line in the dirt with the large stick. "Then, when you joined the board." She slapped the stick against the palm of her hand.

I reached for her, but she pulled away, dropping the branch. "Calm down so we can talk about this."

"Get away from me!" The nervous woman slapped me across the face and clawed my arms, forcing me to let her go. I released my grip, sparking her to jump back like a wild animal. She started to convulse. Her boot got caught in the large, tangled roots, and she stumbled backward, hitting her head. She thrashed about on the ground before her body went still. I sat her up against the tree's base.

Brienne chose to confess to me about how she used to make money. She gave up the names of her past clients. I never could get her to part from her cell phone long enough for me to get the pictures. I left her against the tree and went to get the phone out of her car when a vehicle pulled up. I hid as I watched Alexis circle Brienne's car and pocket the cell phone.

I traveled east on I-10, away from my father's house. Memories of the summer trip to Lafayette a long time ago with my mother emerged. I opened the glove compartment and took out the wrinkled sketch paper I kept over the years. The faded colored childlike letters were still legible: Lafayette, Baton Rouge, New Orleans, Biloxi/Gulfport, Mobile, Pensacola.

I accelerated the Range Rover as I approached the Atchafalaya Basin bridge. I pressed the gas pedal to the floor, escalating the odometer to 90mph, 100mph.

CHAPTER 28

CHELSEA

"Hey," I opened the door. "I'm surprised to see you." Ian hadn't responded to my message, suggesting we take a break while I handle the crisis with the center.

"Can I come in?" he asked.

"Of course." I stepped aside.

"Why did you text me that?" He raised the stool at the kitchen island.

"I didn't think you would want to deal with this mess."

"Let me decide that." Ian's voice boomed.

"Well-I-just thought-"

He pulled me towards him, wrapping his arms around me. "Your mess is mine, too."

Ian maneuvered carefree through the kitchen, whipping up his mastered Puerto Rican shrimp, creole sauce, and rice dish.

"I promise I'll clean this up." He added another dirty dish to the pile in the sink.

"It's fine." I laughed. "I'm just glad you're here."

"Me, too." Ian stirred the sauce as he leaned over to kiss me.

"This is amazing, sweetie." I licked the sauce off my lips. "You have to make this again."

"My secret ingredient is working." Ian teased.

"Yeah, it is." I laughed. My mother's picture popped up on my cell. "Hey, ma. I'm having dinner with Ian."

"Oh, sorry, dear. Call me tomorrow then." Her voice was soft.

"Are you okay?"

"Yeah, I'm fine." She dismissed my concern. "Enjoy your dinner. Stop by tomorrow if you can."

"I'm sorry, sweetie." My mother held my hands in hers. She blamed herself for what Chad did.

"How is this your fault?" I asked.

"The way I handled things back then. He was just a child." She wiped specs of dust off the table and rearranged the flowers in the centerpiece.

"Anyone would have been upset in that situation," I assured. "This is on Dad."

"I agree." Charla chimed in. "He needs to own up to it."

"Your father cut your brother off back then because of things I said."

"What did you say to him?" I asked.

"Things I shouldn't have." My mother sat slumped over in the chair. Dede handed her one of her drawings. "I'll put it on the refrigerator." She squeezed her granddaughter's cheek.

"Y'all didn't even stay together," Charla stated, escorting her daughter back into the living room to watch a show. "Dad had plenty of time to form a relationship with his son." She said, sitting back at the table.

"He was scared of losing his relationship with the two of you." My mother patted Charla on the knee. She looked for a magnet to hang the picture. Dede joined in the search.

Her cell phone dinged, and a message from a man's name that I didn't recognize popped up. Charla tilted her head to the side, motioning to the phone.

"How are things with your job?" I asked.

"My boss swears he doesn't believe it but still put me on indefinite leave." Charla sighed.

"What? Why didn't you tell me?" I questioned. "Is there anything I can do?"

"There's nothing you can do. The company wants to save face."

"Charla, I'm sorry. If you haven't helped me with Haven-"

My sister held up her hand. "I served on the board by choice. You didn't force me."

"Still, that job is your livelihood."

"And I'll find another one." My sister insisted. "Their actions showed it wasn't meant for me anyway."

"You're taking this well."

"I already freshened up my CV and started applying for other jobs."

"You'll find one in no time."

"I know you can do it." Our mother rubbed my sister's back before sitting back down.

"Thanks again for recommending the attorney," I said. "I don't know what I would have done."

"Justin knows him." Charla checked on her daughter, who danced along with the characters on the television. "I thought he would use this against me, but he supported me."

"He knows you're a good mom." Our mother squeezed Charla's hand.

Chad lay in the hospital bed, covered with white sheets and a light blue blanket. He lost control of his vehicle and drove into a barricade on the basin bridge. A nurse at the station said my brother suffered from post-traumatic amnesia. He gave me the once over before picking up the remote.

"Hi, Damien. I mean Chad." I corrected, setting a gourmet snack basket on his bedside table.

My brother laughed at my error. "You were the sweet one." He examined the contents of the basket. I helped him untie the strings. "I remember when you were standing by the staircase next to the other one." He mumbled.

"I don't understand. What do you mean?"

"Your older sister."

"Oh, yes, Charla."

"She didn't want to talk to me." He chuckled. "Holding on to that CD Walkman, turning up her nose at me. She's more like your mother."

"In some ways, I guess." I conceded.

"You wanted to speak to me, but that bitch stopped you."

I ignored how he referred to my mother, remembering the frightened little boy who stood in our home. My mother dared me to speak to him. "I remember. It was the first time I met you and your mom."

I opened a bag of chocolate and mixed nuts, tilting the bag his way.

"Yvette has a way of crashing into places." Chad put some nuts and chocolates in his mouth. "I hate these bare hospital walls." He snapped. "I liked your house. It was much bigger than anything I lived in."

"I grew up in that house. Lots of memories, good and bad."

"Your mom still lives there, not your dad, though; our dad."

"Yes, that's true." I wondered how he knew who lived in our family home.

"I'm sorry that I went after you," he said, "Brienne was my way in." He munched on his snack.

"Do you know what happened to her?" I asked, ignoring the warning of the nurse not to overstimulate. I wanted answers.

He sat up straighter in bed, pushing the sheets off his body. "I-I didn't mean for that to happen. She took some drugs and started fighting me." He rubbed his head. "I tried to calm her down, but she fell." He got quiet, his mind slowing as he lost his train of thought. He grabbed a bottle of water. "I feel like going for a run. Am I a runner?"

The sudden shift in conversation stabbed my heart. The hope of finding out what happened to Brienne slipped away. He waited for a response. "I'm sure you are a runner. You look like one." I smiled.

"Why am I here?" He kneeled in the bed, becoming agitated.

"You were in a bad car accident." I tried to calm him.

"I was in an accident?"

"Yes, and you should take it easy." I touched his arm.

He jerked it away. "Can you get me out of this room? I don't do well in small places."

I felt wet drops trickle down my cheeks. "I'll get the nurse." I bent down and hugged him before pressing the buzzer.

CHAPTER 29

CHARLA

Cindy called me after she left the office. "I have another update for you."

"Okay."

"Aaron only comes in twice a week now. He has permission to work from home."

"I'm not surprised. I told you to request remote approval."

"You know the partners would screw up everything if I weren't there to hold their hand. The office is lost without you, Charla." Cindy sighed.

"I appreciate you saying that."

"Mr. Robichaux had the nerve to ask me to contact you about some reports."

"I know, he called and asked me."

"What did you say?"

"I told him that I didn't want to jeopardize the firm's image by handling business dealings while on leave, and the case is still pending."

"Good for you. Serves him right."

"I'm on my way out, but we'll chat again soon."

"Okay, Charla, talk soon."

I drove to Travis' house to drop off Dede. Chelsea said that Chad could have visitors now, but he was still in ICU. I didn't plan on visiting my half-brother, but I changed my mind after speaking with my sister.

"I like Mr. Travis, momma. He's cool." Dede balanced the iPad in her lap that blasted Kids Bop tunes.

"I like him, too."

Travis approached the car as I pulled into his driveway. His son stood behind him. I put the window down. "Hi, Tristan. Don't you look nice?"

"Hi, Ms. Charla." He hid his face behind his father's leg.

"Stop being so shy." Travis coaxed him.

"Hey, thank you again for watching Dede," I said.

"You know it's not a problem. Tristan is happy to have a playmate." He ruffled the top of his son's head.

"Come on, Dede, get your things." ICU had a short visiting window.

My daughter put the iPad in her backpack before zipping it close and unbuckled her seatbelt. Tristan smiled when Dede got out of the car. She leaned in the car window to kiss me on the cheek before running into the house with her little friend.

Travis touched my arm. "It'll be fine. Call or text me if you need."

"I will. Thank you."

Ever since I gave birth to Dede, I couldn't stand hospitals: the eerie air, odd smells, and constant beeping of life-monitoring equipment. The elevator door opened, and I stepped onto the ICU floor. I reached Chad's room shortly after passing the empty nurses' station. I wondered if his room assignment had anything to do with the severity of his condition. The television screen brightened the dark room.

Chad slept between the bed guard rails, the covers wrapped tightly around his body. I breathed a sigh of relief. The fragile man was nothing like the Damien Brown I encountered in board meetings. Layers of gauze protected his head, and the gentle rhythmic movement of his chest was serene, untroubled by his vengeful actions. I wondered to what extent the post-traumatic amnesia affected his memory. The dangling tubes connected to the mobile machines urged me to yank them, force him to wake up and face me. I ran my fingers down one of them. Chad stirred, slowly opening glassy bright eyes before shutting his lids again. I jumped back.

"Hello, are you family?" A nurse rushed in.

I didn't answer immediately, moving out of her way. "Uhm, uhm, yes. We're related."

"Okay, don't mind me. I just need to check his vitals." The nurse walked over to the other side of the bed by the patient monitor. She wrote her notes on a board on the wall before excusing herself for the night.

Chad moved again. "You're the older one."

That is how he remembered me. "Yes, I am."

"I'm surprised you came." He put the pillow in his lap. "Is your mother with you?" He asked, forcefully fluffing it before putting it back down.

"No, she's not here."

"Good." He got settled. "Can you pour me some water?"

"Sure." My hands shook as I tilted the plastic pitcher over the cup. I moved the table closer to his bed.

"Have a seat." He commanded.

The chair was stiff and unwelcoming. "I don't expect you to like my mother. Not after what happened." The word "bastard" came to mind, and a scared little boy tugged at my father's pant leg before they walked out of the house.

"I'm not the only one who doesn't like her." Chad laughed a private joke.

"She means well." I defended.

"I'm sure she taught y'all that." He turned on his side, his back to me.

"You don't like any of us, do you?"

"I don't really know y'all."

"Why did you do it?" His memory seemed to be on track.

"What did I do to you?" He snapped.

"You don't remember?" I wondered if he forgot or was being cruel.

He rubbed his bandaged head. "I don't remember a lot of things. My other sister said I was in an accident. Did I hit your car or something?" He slowly turned toward me.

"No, you didn't hit me," I said sharply. "You hit the barrier on the bridge."

"For real?" He rubbed his chin. I don't remember that, just that I got hurt."

"Yes, it was a bad accident, but they said you have a good chance at fully recovering."

"I'm glad to hear it." Chad smiled.

"I'll let you get some more rest. I know it's late, and visiting hours are almost over."

"Thanks," he said, pulling the covers up to his chest and picking up the television remote. "What's your name again?"

"Charla, the older one," I said before I wished him goodnight.

CHAPTER 30

CHAD

I slammed the book shut, tossing it at the end of the bed, before hitting the buzzer.

"Where is my cell phone?"

"It's in the closet in your bag with your clothes, Mr. Brown."

"Alright," I grumbled.

"Do you need someone to get it for you?"

"I got it."

The battery died, but the nurse was kind enough to loan me her charger. I scrolled through the notifications, not recognizing some senders and clicking on the important ones. Yvette stuck out among them. That was a name I wished to forget, but no collision was hard enough to give me the pleasure. She called me ten times and sent just as many messages. I cleared her notifications for now and moved on to the others. I heard a knock on the door.

"It's about time. I'm hungry." I called out.

A figure of a man appeared. It was my father and not hospital staff with a tray of half-bland food. He had a brown paper bag in his hand. It had a dark, moist spot from the heat of the food it contained.

"I know they don't feed you real food around here." He handed me the bag.

I slid the plastic water pitcher and cup aside. "Thanks." I took out a breakfast sandwich, hash browns, and orange juice. I handed my father the remote. "Watch something while I eat."

He turned on the TV, grunting as he plopped down on the chair. I paused on a morning news show. I finished off the hash browns before unwrapping the sandwich. I remember he took me out that summer day to get a burger, fries, and shake. He still dressed like a school principal.

"I remember that SUV you had back in the day," I said between bites.

"Yeah." He leaned forward. "It lasted me a long time, too."

"I wanted to be like you," I confessed. "Back then."

"It's natural to want to be like your father." Charles boasted.

"Dropping by once or twice when I was a kid doesn't make you a damn father." I slammed the bottle down. He switched to an investigative crime show. "I can still picture you and Yvette arguing in front of that big two-story house."

"Who can forget it?" He grumbled.

"Do you regret it?"

"What?"

"Hauling me out of your home like that."

"I regret many things, but it's no use in harping on what we can't change."

177

The bright hospital lamp illuminated the bruises on his face and cut on his lip. "You got in a fight or something?"

He cocked his head back. "Yeah, you could say that. You don't remember doing this?" My father pointed to his face.

"I did that?" I asked, swallowing a chunk of the sausage, egg, and cheese sandwich and chasing it with some juice. "Damn, I guess you made me mad."

The shifting of his weight caused the chair to squeak. "I'm the one that should be mad. Look at what you did."

"What did I do? Please tell me."

"This memory loss, amnesia shit won't work on me, son." He pulled the string on the lamp to turn off the harsh light.

An image of my fist punching his face emerged. "You deserved it."

"You can hate me all you want, but that didn't give you the right to go after my children."

"I did what I did because you didn't claim me as one of your children." I threw the bag and bottle in the trash. "If you want someone to blame, look in the mirror."

He struggled to get out of the chair before stepping closer to the bed. "I'm sorry for not taking you in as a kid, but I didn't have a choice back then."

"Yes, you did." I rolled my eyes. "You were the man in that house. Instead, your wife had you acting like a little bitch!"

He gripped the bed rail, his tremoring hand trying to steady himself. "I don't care what I did; you're going to respect me!" He commanded.

"I lost all respect for you years ago, old man." I pushed the hospital tray in the corner.

He grabbed me. "Let go of me," I said. I felt a sharp pain in the back of my head. I rubbed the tight gauze.

He released me, untangling himself from the tubes. I shook my body loose as he moved away. "I could have never worked with your mother to raise you. You lived with her. You know how she is."

"Yes, I do! That was all the more reason for you to fight for me." I yanked the covers. "Just get out of here!"

He hesitated. "I don't want you to ruin your life because of what I did. I don't know how this will play out, but you're young and can start over."

"Is this what you call fatherly advice?" I shrugged off his words.

He opened the door, letting in the sharp light from the hallway. "I hope that one day you and I can talk like a real father and son. Put all this behind us."

"I'm not that little kid you abandoned. I've been taking care of myself all these years. I don't need a dad now. You have a family to care for, remember?"

He closed the door behind him. My head pounded. I stood up and got the cup of water from the tray, stumbling back to the bed. I felt light-headed. The hospital ceiling got fuzzy, and the room started to shrink. There was a tight pain in my chest. I took slow, deep breaths and reached for the nurse's button on the guard rail.

JULY 2024

A family of three sat on a blanket in the park. Their child played with a doll, talking and playing with its hair. The mother gave the little girl a cup that she quickly put in her mouth. The woman took two bottles from a bright-colored ice chest and handed one to the father. He poured water on his head, waiting for her to turn around before splashing her with the rest.

"That's freezing!" The woman yelled, reaching for him, making their daughter laugh.

The toddler got up and wobbled over to hug and kiss her wet parents before dashing toward the large tree with the mysterious large roots.

"No!" Her mother called out. "Stay by Mommy and Daddy." She swooped the child up in her arms, carrying the kicking arms and legs back to the blanket, away from the tree where Brienne died.

The relentless sun beamed the pavement. The hot, stuffy air made it hard to breathe. My toes burned inside my steamy shoes. I wiped my glistening face and squeezed the drenched shirt. Sweat was trapped under my watch, and the weather forecast showed the temperature would spike to over one hundred degrees by midday. I ended this morning's run as I jogged past the peaceful row of multicolor townhomes, turning the corner to enter my complex. I reached my building and started up the stairs when my friendly neighbor appeared.

"Hey!" She sang, locking her door. "I haven't seen you in a while."

"Work keeps me pretty busy." I leaned against the wall. "I travel often."

"What do you do?"

"Cyber security and some freelance."

"That's the thing nowadays. I'm in pharmaceutical sales."

"Nice!" I complimented. "That's some good money."

"It pays the bills." She laughed. "I'm going on a grocery run. Need anything?" She brushed past me, heading down the stairs.

"Uh, no, I'm good, but thanks."

"I wish I were disciplined like you; then I wouldn't have to worry about what I eat."

"I have my struggles." I patted my stomach. "You look fine to me."

"Aw, thanks. You're so sweet."

My attorney sent a notification asking for us to meet. "Nice chatting with you," I said before continuing my climb. "Ice cold water is calling my name."

"Yes, of course. This heat is brutal. Nice running into you." She called out, disappearing down the stairs.

I threw the soaked shirt into the washing machine and chugged a bottle of electrolyte water while I searched for a meal. "Damn." I was out of bread. I cracked some eggs in a pan. I grabbed a bag of grits and slices of turkey bacon.

I put the dirty dishes in the sink when my cell rang. "Hey, I'm about to hop in the shower."

"K, just checkin' on you." Yvette's chipper voice spoke into the phone. "You finished your run?"

"Yeah, just did." I exhaled loudly.

"I know it's hot out there."

"It is." I sighed.

"Make sure you stay hydrated," Yvette ordered.

"That's what I'm doing right now." I opened another bottle of water.

"I'm glad you doin' better." She paused. "I really am."

"I feel like my old self again." I put her on speaker while I stretched my legs.

"I worry about you. You're all I have." My mother got emotional. "Your Aunt Lyn asked about you." She sniffed. "Is this my fault?"

"I don't think we should get into that." I turned on the shower.

"If you ever need to talk, I'm here, k?" Yvette spoke calmly.

"Thanks. I appreciate that." I kicked off my pants. "I'll reach out more."

"I would love that."

I took in the smell of the new SUV's leather seats. The tinted windows and upgraded features in the BMW faded memories of the totaled Range Rover. I selected an R&B rotation playlist before driving off the complex lot.

A few bundles of fallen branches were stacked neatly at the end of driveways, waiting for pick-up. Recent storms left their mark. The humble homes on my father's street kept their front lawns neat. I parked curbside a couple of houses down from my father's. Chelsea drove past me and pulled into the driveway behind Charla. My little niece skipped around the front yard, a sheet of paper flapping in her hand. My father stepped out, bending down to welcome my niece into his arms. He held her paper up and then pressed it against his chest. He gripped the door frame as he got back on his feet and motioned for my sisters to come into the house.

There was a knock on the window. "You lost or something?" The sweaty man held a weed eater.

"No." I lowered the window. "GPS isn't always reliable." I pointed to the screen.

"Right. I keep my directions in here." He pointed to his head. "Have a good one." The eager man went back to edging his lawn.

I drove past my father's home and jumped on the Thruway. I wanted to catch the professor before she left for her weekly brunch.

Made in the USA
Columbia, SC
06 October 2024

43785777R00109